THE ROAD TO
Wherever

BY JOHN ED BRADLEY

For Young Readers
Call Me by My Name
The Road to Wherever

For Adults
Tupelo Nights
The Best There Ever Was
Love & Obits
Smoke
My Juliet
Restoration
It Never Rains in Tiger Stadium

THE ROAD TO Wherever

JOHN ED BRADLEY

FARRAR STRAUS GIROUX
NEW YORK

Farrar Straus Giroux Books for Young Readers
An imprint of Macmillan Publishing Group, LLC
120 Broadway, New York, NY 10271

1 2 3 4 5 6 7 8 9 10

mackids.com

Library of Congress Cataloging-in-Publication Data
Names: Bradley, John Ed, author.
Title: The road to wherever / John Ed Bradley.
Description: First edition. | New York : Farrar Straus Giroux Books for
    Young Readers, 2021. | Audience: Ages 10–14. | Audience: Grades 4–6. |
    Summary: With his father absent and his mother working, eleven-year-
    old Henry "June" Ball must spend the summer on the road with his
    cousins, "Ford men" who repair old cars.
Identifiers: LCCN 2020039321 | ISBN 9780374314057 (hardcover)
Subjects: CYAC: Automobiles—Maintenance and repair—Fiction. |
    Cousins—Fiction. | Fathers and sons—Fiction.
Classification: LCC PZ7.B72466 Ro 2021 | DDC [Fic]—dc23
LC record available at https://lccn.loc.gov/2020039321

Our books may be purchased in bulk for promotional, educational,
or business use. Please contact your local bookseller or the Macmillan
Corporate and Premium Sales Department at (800) 221-7945, ext. 5442,
or by email at MacmillanSpecialMarkets@macmillan.com.

For Kim and Hannah

THE ROAD TO
Wherever

ONE

I REALLY DON'T WANT TO GO, but Mama says I have no choice. She needs to be at the salon all day cutting hair, and there's no way she can afford a sitter.

"I could leave you by yourself," she says, "but all you'd do is play video games and eat. Cold mac and cheese, my chocolate-covered raisins. You know it's true, June. Sorry, bud. Sending you with them really is best for both of us."

I guess it's one more thing to be mad at Daddy about. I'd call him and let him hear about it if only I knew where he was.

Mama and I are at the pizza place next door to the Déjà Do, where she rents a booth. I'm a nice size for eleven and would love to know why she had to order the medium cheese when the large cheese is only a few dollars more.

"I could sweep up the hair," I say. "I could fold the towels. Anything. You don't have to pay me. Just don't make me go, Mama."

"What would my clients think? A big boy like you. Oh,

June." She's trying to sound cheerful all of a sudden. "You'll get to see the country. Isn't that exciting? You don't know it yet, but they're giving you a gift. The mountains and the rivers? The fields that run on forever? Those trees that get so big they cut holes in the trunk so cars can drive through?"

It's a mystery why she makes everything sound like a question. It must be because life comes at her that way—without the answers, ever.

"But they're psychos," I tell her. "They look like Civil War reenactors, and not ones for the good side, either."

"They are not psychos. Take that back, please. They're very fine men who want to make the world a better place."

"Psychos," I repeat, so loud the diners next to us turn to look.

I reach across the table and grab her phone. The restaurant has free Wi-Fi, and I punch up the website for Ball Garage. The site is as rinky-dink as they come, with a picture of Larry and Cornell Ball standing next to a jalopy and the number to call if you need them. Behind them is the building where they fix cars. I know the place because it's in the town where I live, Sheboygan Falls, Wisconsin, and my bus drives by it to and from school each day.

"Look at 'em, Mama. And be honest, come on. They don't scare you just a little?"

"Not me," she says, and pulls the phone out of my hand. She drops it in her purse and zippers the top shut before I can get at it again.

4

Mama claims I've met them before—once at a restaurant in town, another time at church, maybe when I was still a baby. I must've blocked it out of my mind, not wanting to believe I could be related to such people.

She's also explained how they're family, and I repeat it now only because you need to know. A long time ago there were three brothers, and they each got married and had a son. So that made the sons first cousins. Their names were Larry Ball, Cornell Ball, and Henry Ball. Larry and Cornell grew up without ever getting married and having kids, but Henry did marry and have a kid. Henry married my mom and they had me, Henry Junior, which makes Larry and Cornell my cousins, too. Mama says they're my first cousins once removed. I guess it's possible, not that it's something I care to advertise.

"June, honey, they welcome the chance to get to know you," Mama is saying. "They grew up with your dad. And they were thrilled when I asked them to take you on the road with them. It really touched my heart to hear how sweet they were about it. I cried so hard out of relief and gratitude I got raccoon eyes from my mascara running."

"You cried? Over those dudes?"

It must be true, because there she goes doing it again, the tears plowing trails in her makeup even as her little yellow teeth rip into more pizza.

"How long, Mama?" I ask her. "How long do I have to go with them? Please tell me it's not the whole summer."

We're down to the last slice, and I let her have it, hoping she'll think well of me and cut me a break.

"A month, maybe two." Mama's got big football shoulders, and she gives them a shrug. "They want to see how it goes before they commit long term. I'm sure they're as nervous about leaving with you as you are about leaving with them."

"Did you just say two? Two months?"

"It could be that. It could also be the whole summer, although I'm not sure I could stand being away from my little buddy that long."

Her little buddy, huh? But I'm still getting the boot.

It's almost more than I can bear sometimes.

When the time comes I don't pack much, mainly because I don't have much. Mama pulls one of Daddy's old travel bags out of the shed. He got it in the army, and it has his name in stenciled lettering, and when I see the words there, white against the green, I swear I don't know if I should bawl or grab a Sharpie and blot them out.

Mama opens the bag and uses one of her hair-dryers to blow out the dead bugs, then she holds the top open and I start throwing things in: shoes, jeans, shorts, T-shirts, a bunch of underwear. Toiletries like my comb and toothbrush and cherry ChapStick. She says I should also bring some reading material, and she leaves the room and comes back with a small stack of books she found at a thrift shop. They're held together with a rubber band, and all but one are Dork Diaries.

"No way, Jose," I say.

"What's wrong with them? Aren't they for kids your age?"

"For *girls* my age. Boys don't read that stuff."

"They're about dorks. There aren't any boy dorks?"

"If there are I don't want to know about them. What's that other one?"

She pulls it out of the stack. "*The Red Pony* by John Steinbeck," she says. "Are you too good for horses, too?"

Mama isn't letting me take any electronic devices like her phone or the family laptop, so I'm fine with the book. I throw it in the bag. What's wrong with the pony to make it red? I wonder. Did it get blood all over it? I doubt that I'll read enough to find out, but a book might come in handy to hide my face in if my so-called cousins get to prying.

Mama will tell you I'm addicted to video games, but that's just another unfair fabrication. She screams, "Oh, no, you don't!" every time she sees me sitting in front of the TV. If she bothered to check she'd know that a lot of the time I don't even have the video player on. Instead I'm on YouTube watching reunion videos. You know the kind. They're the ones where kids are surprised by absent parents, most of them war veterans who've been away from home a long time.

My favorite is the one where an army dad turns up at his son's school during an assembly. The kid thinks the dad is in Afghanistan, but there he is in the gym. Everybody at the school seems to be in on the surprise but the kid. The moment he sets eyes on the dad, the kid takes off running. He leaps into his dad's arms, and they fall to the shiny floor and roll around while the band plays and people in the bleachers stand and applaud. Everybody bawls, too, even the principal. I must've watched it a thousand times.

Daddy and I never had a reunion like that. He left the army in 2015 after thirteen hard years as a Ranger, and we fled the base in Georgia and moved back home to Wisconsin. I had a lot of friends in Fort Benning, but it's been harder to make friends in Sheboygan Falls. I could blame the kids for not accepting me, but it's really been my fault. The mental health professional at my school told Mama I have anger issues. Mama told her no, I only had a bad temper, inherited from her side of the family. But anybody whose dad is as messed-up as mine would be mad, and anybody would have his guard up about trusting somebody new.

I stopped dreaming about starring in a reunion video with Daddy a long time ago. Now all I want is to see him again.

If he could just walk through the door and tell me to go get the ball so we can throw some passes. Or if he could just sit on the couch and tell me to get him something to drink—a Coke or a glass of water, it doesn't matter, as long as it isn't beer. And for him to reach for my hand as I move past him. And to smile at me the way he used to.

TWO

MAMA HAS TO WORK LATE, but she gets home in time to see me off. We put the porch light on and sit outside, looking past the trash cans on Hickory Street. She's in her chair, and I take the one Daddy always sat in. He'd watch the cars pass by and see how many tall boys he could obliterate, quiet until somebody made the mistake of waving at him.

"You think you know me?" he'd shout. "You don't know me."

He never talked about the war, but it never seemed to leave his mind. He was deployed to Iraq even before I was born, then he went to Afghanistan several times when I was little. They'd send him on secret missions where he parachuted into enemy territory and took out high-value targets. Mama would never tell me who those targets were, but it was because of these missions that Daddy got PTSD. PTSD stands for post-traumatic stress disorder. It's when you can't get a terrifying event out of your head and you think about it so much it makes you kind of nuts and it feels like the event is happening all over again.

That was Daddy. You could be talking to him about the Packers and he would start crying. "Oh God," he'd say. And you knew then to go to your room. Other times he'd start cursing, his voice getting louder until he was screaming. And then up and down the street all the other porch lights would be popping on.

Now I keep wondering if Larry and Cornell will understand that cheese is not a sometimes thing for me. And I wonder if they'll get it when I tell them I don't welcome questions, especially ones about my personal life.

"Why don't we wait until tomorrow?" I tell Mama out on the porch.

"No, bud."

"But nothing they do makes sense. Traveling at night? Why do they have to travel at night like a couple of vampires when they can travel during the day like normal people?"

"Cooler at night. Less traffic."

"They don't get sleepy?"

"If one gets sleepy, he surrenders the wheel to the other one. That way the driver is always rested and alert. Makes perfect sense to me."

"What if they both get sleepy?"

"They stop for some coffee or Red Bull. Or they pitch their tent in the woods and take a nap. Sometimes—Cornell told me this—one will holler at the other one until he wakes up. He said it works. I also think they're the kind of people who don't need much sleep. They've got work to do—important work—and there is not a minute to waste."

"I'd hate to slow them down, Mama."

"You're their first stop this year, bud. Gosh, what an honor. And how humbling for me as a parent."

For a while the only sound I hear is our chairs squeaking, but then at around ten o'clock the low rumble of an engine finds us, and I see headlights up ahead turning the neighbor's lattice fence into a golden honeycomb. Next an ancient box truck appears on the street and slows to a stop in front of the house. The truck might've been red fifty years ago, before fading to a pinkish brown. The front end looks like a pug expressing its displeasure at the frog it just ate. Daddy took me once to the antique car show at River Park, but I don't remember any old tanks like this one. The tall light at the head of the driveway burns yellow, and when the truck turns in, I see this word written on the side of the box in back: *Ford*.

Mama stands before I do. She runs out to greet them, and the three of them give each other fake kisses in the headlights.

Is this where I look around and start memorizing things, in case I never make it back home? I wish there was a cat or a dog to say goodbye to, but Mama won't let me have one.

"An animal?" she likes to say. "How can I feed an animal when I can barely afford to feed you?"

It is only a week since school let out. Next time somebody tells you life isn't fair, you have my permission to mention my name.

THREE

THEY'RE BOTH TALL AND SKINNY—whip-thin, Daddy would've called them. And they both have goatees that reach down to their belly buttons and seem to serve as apologies for their shiny bald heads. Each one is wearing blue coveralls with a Ford logo patch on the right sleeve and *Ball Garage* in raised letters across the back. Their brown leather boots are stained with oil droplets and paint drips.

"June?" Mama says. "What on earth are you waiting for, bud? Let's go. Grab your bag and come over here. Your cousins are waiting."

I shuffle over and extend my hand to make sure they understand that a hug or a kiss is not going to happen.

"June," Larry says, squeezing my finger bones so hard I almost scream. He glances over at Mama. "He's grown into quite the specimen, all right."

"Oh, yeah," Mama says. "June's never been one to miss a meal. Got that from me. If the schoolbooks don't pan out in his future, he could always be a competitive eater. The child can flat put it away."

Larry is the older one. He's taller than Cornell, though not by a lot. Also, his beard is longer and not as wiry. It's also possible that his head shines more, I suppose because he sweats more. Like Cornell, his name is scripted in red thread over his pocket. I am grateful that their names are on their clothes. Without them I'd always be having to measure their beards and sweat to tell one from the other.

"How exciting to have you joining us," Cornell says, when it's his turn to shake. I'm prepared this time, but it doesn't hurt any less. I'm thinking he might've crushed a knuckle, the one on my favorite finger.

I should confess now that I don't like my name. First Mama and Daddy were calling me Henry Junior, then it was just Junior, since Daddy was already Henry. Then somehow I morphed into June Bug. There were June bugs galore in Georgia, but I hated the name so much that I took to throwing things every time Mama and Daddy called me that—an alarm clock, a mango, a giant bowl of Neapolitan ice cream. After a while they realized it was going to be expensive unless they shortened it to June, even though anybody will tell you that June is a girl's name.

June Ball . . . I mean, what were they thinking? How could they do that to me?

"Where are we going?" I say, standing in the light from the truck. "Can you tell me that much at least?"

Larry removes a little notebook from his pocket and starts turning the pages. These pages are full of scribbles with phone numbers and street addresses and arrows pointing every which way. I also see pictures of birds and flowers and animals. A squirrel and a rabbit. Maybe a newt. His lips move, but I can barely hear what he's saying. It might be the names of cities and towns. It also might be the names of people. Even as he's reading, the phone in his pocket is humming and dinging. People with Fords, you have to think.

If you go to Google and type in *Ford men*, you'll find a few stories about these two. Or you can just go to YouTube and have a look at the story a TV station in Milwaukee did a few years ago.

It's the one where a reporter lady caught up with them on a job. The car came out of a barn, and Larry and Cornell had it in a field where some cows were grazing, and this old farmer-looking dude was standing back a ways, watching, and the lady points to Cornell's sleeve and says, "That blue oval with the word *Ford* in it means the world to these crackerjack mechanics. Larry and Cornell Ball are Ford men, and every time they encounter that familiar logo they tingle from head to toe.

"Why Fords? The answer is simple: The Ball family has been associated with the car company dating back generations. A vehicle like the 1932 Coupe they're repairing today, one of this vintage and rarity, has the cousins feeling a moral obligation to it. God in heaven created them to keep classic

Fords running, and so each summer, they hit the road in search of heaps to fulfill that task. Larry and Cornell Ball own Ball Garage in Sheboygan Falls, but more important, they belong to the cult of the blue oval, and they've given their souls to it. Not Chevy, mind you. And not Studebaker or Nash or even the elusive Tucker. For the Ball cousins, it's Ford and Ford alone.

"Do you own a Country Squire that needs to be brought back from the grave? What about a Fairlane convertible? If these gentlemen find out about it, they are likely to show up on your doorstep asking what they can do to help."

Mama watched the video with me the other night. When it was over she said, "I wish your daddy had been a Ford man instead of an army man."

I didn't say anything, and she took the thumb and forefinger of her right hand and pressed them against her eyes to stop the tears from escaping. "Loving him wasn't a mistake because we have you. But he sure has made it difficult. Lord help me, June. I must've been out of my mind to ever say, 'I do.'"

FOUR

HE LEFT ON A SUNDAY MORNING four months ago, when snow was still on the ground. I peeked out the window and smiled at him as he was warming his pickup. I wish I could remember the last thing he said to me. It might offer a clue to where he was going. But I can't bring back a single word.

He was often wonderful. You should also know that. Catch him when his mind was right and he wasn't drinking, and nobody was better. He took me fishing, and he took me on a tour of Lambeau Field, the stadium in Green Bay where the Packers play. He watched kids' movies I knew he hated just for the chance to sit next to me on the couch. Nobody should ever say he deserted us—the man was no deadbeat. I might not get why he left, but he wouldn't have done it unless he had to. And he hasn't called or come back because he can't yet. He would if he could, but he can't, so we just need to be patient and wait. Please don't get to thinking the wrong things about him. Or that I hate him.

The morning he left, Mama and I went to church by ourselves. When we got home I checked out back, thinking he might've been in his shop, but he wasn't there. In the house I went from room to room looking for him. I even checked the closets. "Daddy?" I said each time I pulled a door open.

Mama baked a chicken while I cleaned the porch, throwing his beer cans from the night before into a tall kitchen bag. I stopped counting at seventeen empties. Mama set the table and piled his plate high with all the things he liked: drumsticks, stuffing, broccoli, creamed corn, a dinner roll. It stayed on the table the whole day until she gave up and added it to the bag with the cans.

That night before I went to bed I had one more look outside. You could still see his prints in the snow, leading from the porch to where he always parked.

The truth is, I don't know a Ford from a hole in the ground. I'm not even sure what kind of pickup Daddy drives. It could be a Ford. I'm not saying it isn't. But just as easily it could be something else.

A Mercedes, a Volvo, a Maserati. I mean, what do I know?

"Forgive my ignorance, but what kind of kooky truck is this, anyway?" I say now to the two freaks standing in my yard.

"It's a Ford COE truck," the one named Cornell answers, pronouncing the word so it rhymes with Joe. "COE stands for cab-over-engine. See how the cab sits over the engine? This one dates to 1948. Cousin Larry and I are purists, meaning we like to keep things as we find them, but we did add the big container on the chassis in back. We needed a lot of storage space, for our tools and whatnot. See how Larry painted *Ford* on the sides? Did that himself. A little crooked, but so what? The truck is gorgeous, ain't it, June?"

At first I think he's joking, but the more I study his expression the more I think otherwise.

Mama doesn't seem to have been listening. "June really likes his cheese," she says. "American cheese, cheddar cheese, Gouda, feta, Monterey Jack, cottage, cream, mozzarella—"

"Are you going to name all the cheeses, Mama?"

"If you reach a point where you don't know what to feed him, stop at 7-Eleven and see if they have any Kraft Easy Cheese. Comes in a bottle. Tip his head back and squirt some in his mouth, and you've never seen somebody so happy."

Larry and Cornell are staring at me like zombies. All manner of flying insects cut circles around them, but they don't seem to mind. I have this urge to run, but where would I go? The woods? I hate the woods, especially at night.

The engine's still running and the doors are open, and from inside, banjo music is playing on a little transistor radio stuck with a strip of silver duct tape to the middle of the dashboard. I notice the driver's door decorated with these words: *Larry Ball, Artist*. And these on the other one: *Cornell Ball, Studio Assistant*.

They must think that's cute. But I'm seeing their names on those doors and I'm thinking, since I have to go with them, that they should add mine now, only it would say: *June Ball, no one and nobody.*

"We added a seat belt for you," Larry says. "See there in the middle? It was important we do that, not that we've ever had an accident, knock on wood." He leans over and raps a fist of knuckles against the side of Cornell's head.

I remember the words Daddy used to yell when he couldn't take it anymore. I could start yelling them now. But instead I decide to stare at Mama. I'm trying to communicate telepathically that she ranks among the worst mothers of all time for what she's about to make me do.

"Think you'll like camping under the stars, June?" Larry asks. "Drinking and bathing out of a hose?"

He must think kids enjoy that kind of stuff.

"Not to hurt your feelings or anything, but, no, I don't think I will."

Larry is undeterred. I think that's the correct word. "What about waking up each morning to the sizzle of bacon and eggs frying in a cast-iron skillet? Butter biscuits baking in a Dutch oven? Farm-fresh butter and blackberry jam?"

"Throw in a slice of Velveeta and he might," Mama says.

Larry isn't finished listing things I can look forward to. "What about digging a privy? What about *using* it? Think you'll be okay with that?"

"A privy?" Mama says. "That's an outdoor toilet, correct?" And she scrunches up her face like the wind just changed directions and brought a smell with it.

"That's correct, dear," the cousins answer, both at once.

"Why can't we just use the bathroom in the house?" I say.

"What house?" Larry says.

"The house with the Ford."

"Not always a house around," Larry says. "And we wouldn't want to do that to our friends anyway, would we, June?"

They're friends now? How are people they don't know their friends? Just because they own crummy Fords?

"Where are we going?" I ask again, quieter but more desperate now.

"Wherever we are needed," Cornell answers, while Larry nods as if he just heard some words carved in stone.

Cornell tosses my bag in the back of the truck before I can climb up in there and have a look around. This really bothers me because I can tell I'm going to need the horse book. Then he and Larry shuffle over to Mama and fake more kisses. What a show they put on, and all at my expense.

Mama's getting emotional. You can even see her nose starting to drip. It's leaving little wet dots on her muumuu.

Both Larry and Cornell reach for the shop cloths in their back pockets. Mama starts howling now—it's more like I died than I'm leaving. She unloads into one cloth and then destroys the second one, and next thing she's got me in her arms and she's squeezing so tight I honestly worry I might have an accident in my pants.

"Not my baby," she says, obviously forgetting that it was her idea in the first place. "You're *taking* him? You're taking my baby?"

"Cool it, Mama. Come on. Too late for all that."

Finally Larry and Cornell grab her arms and pull back hard enough to break her grip, and I escape and run around to the passenger side. I climb up on the seat and slide over to the middle, where there's a long stick shift poking up. I straddle the thing, a leg on each side.

"I'm going to miss you, bud," Mama whimpers.

I almost yell back, "You will?" real sarcastic-like, but it wouldn't do any good. I'm going. And in a way I can't explain, this trip I'm about to take feels like it really began four months ago. That's when I walked back in the house and Mama, sniffling on the couch, shoved another handful of chocolate-covered raisins in her mouth and said, "It must be really bad this time, June. It's not like your dad to cut out on my baked chicken."

Out by the truck now she uncorks one last scream: "*Juuuuuuune!*" Like I just that minute got hit in the road.

"Bye, Mama." I crunch my fingers against the heel of my palm the way some girls at school do when a regular wave isn't cute enough.

We reverse onto Hickory Street, and Larry watches in the side mirrors. He leans forward against the steering wheel. "Did you remember to pack the eggs, cousin?" he says.

Cornell shoots a thumb in the direction we're going, which is backward. I don't know how it answers the question, but Larry smiles and seems satisfied.

On the way out of town we pass by Ball Garage. Larry punches the horn and lets out a whoop. Junky cars are parked in front, rows of yellow-green lights shining down on them. I count five closed garage doors along the side of the building facing the road, each with a blue oval painted on it. Out behind the building are a pair of small travel trailers. They are older models with rounded bodies clad in polished aluminum.

"Airstreams," Larry says. "That one there with the petunias by the door is Cornell's. The other one with the begonias is mine."

He's pointing, but I can't tell which is which because I don't know my flowers and the trailers look exactly alike. "You go camping in those things?"

"No, June. We live in them. Those are our houses."

"All the modern conveniences, including running water and a flush toilet," Cornell says. He sticks an arm out the window and gives a crazy wave. "Bye, house. See you when we get back."

"Bye, house," Larry says, tooting the horn again. "Love you, house. Wish us well in our travels, house."

Man, oh, man, is all I can think.

They keep the windows down and let the air pour in, and it feels pretty good for air that's not coming from an air conditioner. It's dark inside. I see now why they taped the radio to the dash. The truck doesn't have one, which makes you wonder if radios were even invented back when this clunker was built. On the dash there are assorted gauges under glass, but none are digital. The truck doesn't even have cruise control. No lights anywhere. No cup holders. I suppose when you buy some coffee you have to hold it between your legs. The way we're bouncing around, that could lead to an emergency room visit.

The radio keeps playing the same cornball stuff that I finally remember the name for: bluegrass. But the station is getting staticky, so Cornell thumbs the dial and finds a new one: two guys talking Brewers baseball. It makes sense. We're driving through Milwaukee now, the city spread out on either side of us.

Larry and Cornell stare straight ahead, and it seems the road has them hypnotized. The reflectors on the centerline keep coming at us, and you can see them in the mirrors of their shiny bald heads.

"Road turtles," I say. "That's what Daddy calls them. Those reflectors? You guys have a name for them?"

"Sure, road turtles," they say.

"Listen, I've been wondering. Aren't all cars basically the same? Aren't they just meant to take you from one place to another? Why does it have to be a Ford?"

The question seems fair, but Larry and Cornell both turn and stare at me. Their goatees are trembling, which tells me their chins must be doing the same.

"I mean, what does it matter if it's a Ford or a Dodge? Or a Ford or a Hyundai? As long as it takes you where you need to go?"

"That jersey you're wearing," Larry says, squeezing the steering wheel with both hands. "Are the Packers your team, June?"

"Yes, they are."

"And why is that? Why them and not somebody else, like the Bears, say?"

"The Bears? I hate the Bears."

"Okay, all right. But why do you hate them so much? The Bears ever do anything to you?"

"They play the Packers. That's enough right there."

"So you're a Packers man. Loyal to them, win or lose; root for them through thick and thin. When they have a bad game, it's hard to sleep afterward. When the whole season goes bad, nothing's any good until the next season and they get that first win. Well, it's the same general concept for cousin Cornell and myself with automobile companies. We're Ford to the bone, son. You'll never catch a Ball driving anything else."

"Is my dad's pickup a Ford?"

"Henry's? Are you kidding? Of course he drives a Ford. Cornell and I had the pleasure of working on it once, didn't we, cousin?"

"Recored the radiator."

They must've bathed before we left because I smell soap. It's mixed with a slight burned-oil smell coming up from the floor. I look out at the cars and trucks moving past us and try to see faces. I wish one would be my dad's. I wish he'd glance up right as I was glancing down.

"Every young person should experience the American road," Larry says, really out of nowhere. "Cornell and I are delighted that we can be your guides this summer. We have nothing but admiration for your mother and father."

"Okay," I say, not sure how else to answer.

"Henry's truck," Cornell says. "It's a '72 F-100, am I right?"

"Yes," Larry answers. "A Ranger XLT."

A car moves past us on the left. I sit up for a look. "Maybe we'll see them on the way to where we're going," I say. "Daddy and his pickup?"

More trembling goatees, and that is it.

You might be wondering if Larry and Cornell look like my dad. I would have to say no. They look like each other more than they look like him. He doesn't have any facial hair, and he isn't bald. I don't see tattoos on them, either. Daddy has a little bitty one on the inside of his left wrist. From a distance it looks like a couple of warts, but when you get up close you can see it's really words, and the words are *Sua Sponte*, which Daddy said is the Rangers' motto. It means nobody makes them sacrifice so much. They do it because they choose to.

Larry shines a flashlight on his watch. "Midnight," he says. "How about that, June? You made it."

"I stayed up till four once, just to see if I could do it. I wanted to make it to sunup, but I couldn't resist Mama's leftover lasagna and it knocked me out."

Out on the road now, I'm starting to see welcome signs for the state of Illinois. That's nice of Illinois to open their arms to us like that. It's not until we officially leave Wisconsin and enter the Prairie State that Larry and Cornell speak again. Too bad it's more about eggs.

"In the Time Sensitive cooler, correct?" Larry asks.

"Correct," Cornell answers.

"Did you remember about the paprika?"

"Yes. Light on the paprika, just like I always do."

FIVE

WE KEEP GOING.

Going and going.

The next big city is Chicago, and I really should say ginormous, because the size of that place is not to be believed. It's like ten Milwaukees rolled into one. Wherever I look, I see factories, shopping malls, and neighborhoods crowded with houses. Streetlights make the view almost as bright as day. We drive for more than an hour before we get free of it, and even now everything on both sides of the interstate is built up. These are the burbs, Larry says, and it seems there's no end to them. The highway is much busier than I would have expected at this hour. Semis cruise up alongside us for a look at the truck, and the drivers seem to be marveling at the sight. Sometimes they wave, or give a thumbs-up, or toot their air horns. I can tell Larry and Cornell enjoy the attention. I like it, too, even though none of it is my doing.

It's not until we're out in the sticks again that Larry pulls off the road at a rest area. "Need to stretch your legs, June?" he says.

"Need to do more than that."

"Men's room is up there." And he points.

I half limp, half run to the place, wondering if I'll make it.

When I'm done I wash my hands and take my time drying them under one of those wall dryers. Only one of the stalls is occupied, and I look down under the door at the man's shoes. I'm trying to decide if they could be my dad's.

After we got all set up in Sheboygan Falls he found a job working highway construction. They taught him how to drive a grader and a sheepsfoot roller, and he got to wearing Red Wing boots to work. He liked them so much he wore them even on his days off, but what I'm seeing now in the stall are loafers with tassels. No way can I picture Daddy in anything like that, not even if he found an office job.

Something must be wrong with me to think I'm going to find him late at night in a bathroom on the side of the interstate, in a place whose name I don't know, if it even has a name. It's a good thing I come to my senses. I run out of there the second before the dude with the loafers kicks the handle and exits the stall.

Larry and Cornell are sitting side by side at a picnic table not far from the truck. I take it that the bench across from them is reserved for me, and I slide in and lean forward against the concrete top. They're eating deviled eggs, each one decorated with red powder and a green olive slice. The eggs are in a molded tray, and they're putting them away in single bites, as if bothering to eat them in more moderate portions is a waste of time.

"No need to be bashful," I say, thinking they'll get the joke.

But they just look at me, their mouths full, jaws pumping.

"June, would you like an egg?" Cornell says.

"No."

"No, sir," Larry corrects me.

It's not mean, the way he says it. It's not a threat or even a reprimand. It's more like a fact, like this is how it is and how it's going to be.

"No, sir," I say.

I don't know how to explain it, but it feels good to say those words. I haven't said them in a while—four months to be precise.

Larry's phone chirps in his pocket. He looks at it and scribbles in his notebook, then he reaches for another egg. "I do all the scheduling," he says, as if it's perfectly normal that someone is contacting him about a car repair in the middle of the night. "It's a challenge sometimes, but I enjoy dealing with the public. It's also fun getting a call or email from somebody who might have something special and they don't know it yet."

Cornell holds up another egg, this one in the space between us. "Excellent source of protein," he says. "Flavorful. Easy to digest. I'm the camp cook, so I made them myself. Go ahead, June. Have one."

I have a long look at the thing. The yellow stuff in the

middle is disgusting—there's no other word for it—but then I think, *Oh, what the hay*. If it can be the first time I ever got sent out on the road with a couple of oddballs, why can't it be the first time I ever ate a deviled egg?

I take the one he's offering and smell it, which to be honest isn't so great, and then I open my mouth and slide it in. It's a little slimy at first, and I almost upchuck, but Cornell's eyes are pleading with me not to give up. *Be brave*, they are saying. *You can do it.*

"He has a secret ingredient," Larry says. "I'd pay big bucks to know it."

"Tasty, huh?" Cornell says, and makes his eyebrows dance.

Five minutes later we've wiped out the whole tray.

SIX

I DON'T KNOW WHAT CHICKENS put in their eggs to make you sleepy, but the ones I just ate must've been loaded with it. Cornell is taking his turn behind the wheel, and he's talking about how this is his twenty-fifth summer with Larry on the road. When doctors have time off, they go to third-world countries and give free medical care to poor people, he explains. During tornado and hurricane season, carpenters show up at places that have been pulverized and help with the rebuild. "What we do is no different," Cornell says. "Only it's Fords we show up for."

Larry and Cornell sound a lot alike. By that I mean they both have deep voices and a slow, careful way of talking. If my teachers talked like them my head would never get off the desk. I fall asleep as Cornell's explaining how to recore a radiator. I feel my head nod forward and jerk back. I try to hold it upright, but it lobs forward again, and this up-and-down routine goes on for miles until I feel somebody grab me and pull me against him. It's Larry, offering his arm as a pillow.

At one point I come awake, just for a moment, and exhale a breath of hot, eggy air. I'm not sure where I am or even who I am. And it's pitch-black except for a pair of distant headlights on the interstate. I glance up at Larry, and he's looking back with a familiar smile on his face. It's a look I last saw when Daddy carried me to bed after I conked out in front of the TV.

That look they give you, that soft one, I'm not sure what to say about it except that it must be love or something like it, something extremely close.

I don't wake up until we've stopped again. Our headlights are washing over an old van, and Larry's already working on it. It looks like the engine's built into the floor between the two front seats, and he's hovering over it, tools in both hands. Cornell is sitting behind the steering wheel, one leg inside with his foot on the accelerator, the other leg hanging outside. There's something different about the van, and it takes me a while to figure it out: The steering wheel is on the wrong side. It's on the right side instead of the left.

A tall Black man is watching him work. He's wearing a bathrobe and pajamas, both made of the same shiny striped material, and he's drinking from a coffee cup with *Ford* stamped on the side. Every time he breathes, steam pours from his mouth and colors the air in front of his face.

Directly behind him is a collection of metal buildings,

each the size of an airplane hangar. The giant door to only one of the buildings is open, and it's right in front of me. Past the man I can see rows of antique cars, hundreds of them lined up next to one another. Even in the dreamy half-light they shine brighter than new models in a dealer's showroom.

I just now notice the sign over the door. FAIRCLOTH MOTORS, it says.

I could pretend to know what Larry and Cornell are doing—I could say they're cranking the crankshaft or connecting the connecting rod or fibrillating the defibrillator—but eventually my lies would catch up to me, most likely when I least need them to. So let me just say they aren't playing around.

I slide over for a better view off to my left. There's a plane down that way at the end of a landing strip. The strip is all lit up, and the plane's stairs are down, and a guy who must be the pilot is standing out there by himself.

"Okay, try it now," Larry says. His hands are buried deep in the engine, and his voice is urgent. Cornell pumps the gas and turns the key, and the old jalopy whinnies and coughs. I've never actually seen a mule in real life, but the van is acting like one. It's being that stubborn, anyway.

"Again," Larry says. And it's more of the same: *No, no, please don't make me leave the barn!* They do this four or five times before the engine finally starts. The sound smooths out as Larry keeps tinkering. The pajama man holds a fist up, and Cornell cuts the engine.

"My heroes," the man says, and the three of them exchange high fives.

A minute later the man's driving the van into the building and we're heading out on a long cement road that curves between a pair of small hills.

"So that's what you do?" I say. "That's it?"

"Well, yeah, sometimes it is," Larry says. "Most times it takes longer. We've spent weeks on single jobs. Each one is different."

"What kind of Ford was that?"

"That was a Thames 400E, June." It's Larry again. "Ford made it for the British market, so we rarely see them in this country. Did you notice the steering wheel? That tells you it's not American—people in England drive on the left side of the road, thus the different wheel placement. What makes that particular vehicle special is the provenance, which means history of ownership. That was the van the Beatles traveled in from one performance to the next when they were first starting out in the early 1960s. Yes, it was, June. Yes, it was. Do you know who the Beatles were, son?"

"Sure. 'I Want to Hold Your Hand' and all that."

"Mr. Faircloth just had the van delivered all the way from Liverpool. He did this at great expense, only to find that he couldn't get it started. It was a treat to work on that Ford tonight. Wasn't it a treat, cousin?"

"One of the biggest treats of my life. Here"—Cornell offers me his arm—"sleep, June. We have another hour before we have to stop again."

Who has treats anymore? I suppose they do. I don't know why I'm surprised.

We are still southbound on the interstate. I'm really not all that sleepy anymore, but my head's been feeling kind of heavy on my neck, so I go ahead and lean it against Cornell's arm.

I keep seeing this girl from my class last year even though I honestly couldn't stand her. It is bizarre. She's out there in the headlights staring back at me with her lips puckered.

Then I'm seeing my dad, which is even more disturbing. We're walking along the beach at Lake Michigan and throwing little brown rocks at each other, and Mama is yelling for us to cut it out. It really is a wonder one of us doesn't lose an eye, as the baby rocks go sailing by. In this instance Mama is right to be wailing. Every throw misses until one ticks against my face. I yelp even though it doesn't hurt much, and Daddy comes running over. He holds me, laughing and apologizing, and he kisses the spot on my cheek where the rock got me, and his eyes are red and shiny from another long night. What's strange is that the memory carries a smell, and it's the Dentyne he's been chewing to cut his sour beer smell. Poor Daddy. PTSD really is a disease. The beach runs on forever, and the water keeps sending cold waves against our feet.

I don't need to be seeing Daddy or that girl's lips, so I snap out of it and dial up the pajama man. "Is Mr. Faircloth rich?" I say.

Both Larry and Cornell are slow to nod, and when they

do, their heads go up and down at the exact same time. I wonder how they do that. Must take practice.

"And who is he exactly? Not that you need to say. I'm just curious."

"First and foremost, he's our friend, June," Larry says. "He's also the preeminent collector of rare Fords in these United States."

"The whole world," Cornell mutters.

Larry corrects himself: "You're right, cousin. Thank you. The whole world."

"Were all those buildings full of cars, or just that one with the doors open?"

"All of them," Larry says. "Well, no, there's a warehouse for operations—for parts and tools and equipment that Mr. Faircloth's army of mechanics use, and a section where they do general rehab and paint and body work. But all the other buildings hold his collection. He's voracious—he owns thousands of Fords—and it's a pathology with him, a medical situation that he seems unable to cure." Larry chuckles. "He owns so many Fords he stopped counting."

"I know a kid like that with lapel pins."

"Mr. Faircloth will tell you he is not a materialistic person. His goal, he says, isn't to accumulate history but to preserve it. You'd never guess how he started as a collector."

I'm about to come up with something, but Larry stops me. "He owned a nursing home and a patient couldn't satisfy his debt, so the patient offered Mr. Faircloth his car in payment.

The car turned out to be a Ford 2GA, made in the forties during the war. If I recall correctly, Mr. Faircloth said he was driving a new Cadillac Fleetwood Brougham at the time, but it stayed home in the garage each day when he went to work. Instead Mr. Faircloth drove the 2GA. That's when he caught the Ford bug. He still takes the 2GA out on special occasions."

"Crazy," I say, as in crazy good. But of course they take it wrong.

They wait a while before saying anything, I guess to give me time to reconsider my last comment.

"Not the word I would use, but all right," Larry says. "Now whenever a new patient checks into one of Mr. Faircloth's facilities—he owns hundreds of those, too—he asks about the cars they're leaving behind. He's found many fine examples that way."

We go on for another few miles. Something Larry said a minute ago doesn't make sense. "If it's true that Mr. Faircloth has an army of his own mechanics," I say, "then why does he need Larry and Cornell Ball to show up in the middle of the night to get his van started?"

They crack smiles, happy that I've been paying attention. It's Cornell's turn: "Because of our friendship, we have an agreement that's proven to be mutually beneficial. Mr. Faircloth calls us first whenever he makes a new purchase, and in consideration we call him first whenever we find a Ford of historical significance that we think will fit in his collection. He pays for parts or provides them, and he covers the cost of our gas, but that's all we get. We don't bill him for labor, and we never upcharge. Some would regard this arrangement as tipped in his favor, but they don't understand. We would travel the world to be the first hands on a rare find, and he provides us with that experience. These cars are our raison d'être, June. Do you know what that means?"

I think about it. "Something to do with grapes?"

Cornell shakes his head. "It's French for 'reason to be.'"

"Raison d'être," I say, giving it a shot.

"Raison d'être!" they repeat in perfect sync.

SEVEN

CORNELL REMOVES HIS FOOT from the gas and works the clutch and the stick, and the truck begins to slow.

We exit the interstate and follow a ramp to a crossroad. Cornell seems to have miscalculated the distance. He's forced to brake hard as a flashing red light looms up ahead. Larry responds to the quick stop by throwing his left arm in front of me. He's trying to keep me from crashing into the windshield, and I'm fine with it, even though there seems to be some confusion about my age, never mind that I'm belted to the seat.

Larry might not know a little kid from somebody who just shredded fifth grade, but I like that he has my back, or my face in this case.

I couldn't tell you the last time Daddy saved my life.

On the radio the deejay gives ZZ Top a break and announces the time: 6:21 A.M. I wish you could see what I'm seeing. The sun's climbing up out of the ground and shooting through some trees in the distance, and clouds of birds form swarming dot patterns in the sky. Even the dust in the air twinkles with light, and everything looks new and warm and golden. It was only my first night on the road, and now I'm seeing my first sunup. Mama said Larry and Cornell were giving me a gift. I didn't believe her until now.

"Wouldn't you love to be one of those birds?" Cornell says. "They look happy, don't they, June?"

"Oh, man."

"I got a world of respect for birds—how they decorate the landscape with little blips of color and sing while doing it. Gotta love a bird, huh, June?"

"Yes, sir. Nothing like a bird."

As we hang a left, Larry taps his phone with his index finger, and a voice starts giving directions in a foreign accent. It's the GPS navigator.

"Australian," Cornell says before I can ask the question. "From the other side of the globe, but somehow he knows where to go."

We're in western Indiana now, way out in no-man's-land. Fields full of green plants stretch out on either side of the road, broken only by barns and farmhouses. We motor through towns where everything looks dead and sheriff's deputies, waiting for speeders, sleep in their cars under billboards for Walmart and Tractor Supply. It's starting to feel like we'll never get to where we're going when the Australian guy suddenly announces that our destination is ahead on the right. Cornell brakes and shifts and wheels into a parking lot. It's a dusty old diner from a hundred years ago. Letters on the roof spell out the word SCAR'S.

What kind of crazy restaurant goes by the name Scar's? I look more closely. The first of the letters, an O, has come loose from the metal bracket that attaches it to the roof.

Past the windows in front you can see dim lights hanging over a long counter. A man on a stool looks to be the only customer. He's sitting with his head pitched forward. Is he sleeping or licking his plate? Because the light is so bad, it's impossible to tell. A much younger guy in an apron is standing next to him.

Cornell drives around back as Larry reads from his notebook: "Mr. Oscar Alejandro is deceased. Client Nico is his twenty-two-year-old grandson. Nico inherited the diner. Also a '57 Ranchero."

There's a pickup in the lot, but it looks fairly new. Then I spot the bomb parked in the grass just past where the lot ends. Weeds growing up around it are so tall they reach above the door handles.

"That it?" Larry says.

Cornell leans forward against the wheel, squinting.

Larry starts reading again: "Nico couldn't afford to have it towed or worked on at any of the area garages. The Ranchero's been parked in the same spot for three years, and somebody recently walked off with the hubcaps. Nico found our website and thought he'd see if we were for real."

"Anything else?" Cornell says.

"Nico makes excellent pancakes." Larry looks up from the notebook. "Said we should try them even if we can't get the Ranchero running."

Cornell's chuckling and shaking his head as he steps down from the cab. "Can't get it running," he mumbles as if Larry just told a joke.

It's been a long trip, and my body's sore from sitting. Larry and I stand out in the lot doing stretches and running in place while Cornell shuffles over to a back door with a sign that says DELIVERIES ONLY. He slaps it with the flat of his hand. The door cracks open, and Cornell turns sideways, tilting his shoulders just enough to show the back of his coveralls.

"Hey, you made it!" a voice says.

I can smell butter and syrup. The young guy from the counter steps outside. *Soft* might be the best way to describe him: soft body under the apron, soft hair under a Farmall cap turned backward. "I am so impressed," he says. "You're exactly like they said." He brings both hands up and waves to Larry and me.

"Nico, my name is Cornell Ball. That handsome gentleman over there is Larry Ball, and our dashing young compatriot is none other than June Ball."

"Well, welcome to Oscar's, everybody. Thank you for coming. You guys must be starving. Would you like coffee or a bite to eat before you get started?"

"Coffee sounds great," Cornell says. "So does breakfast. But if you don't mind, we'd like a look at the Ranchero first."

My stomach's been growling with the volume cranked, and I almost say, "*We would?*" But then I decide it's no use. They'd only tell me Fords are more important than food.

Nico digs a ring of keys out of his pocket and removes the one for the Ranchero. "Here you go, Mr. Cornell. Just for your information, my grandpa bought it new from Campbell Motors up the road and drove it nearly every day of his adult life. I'll tell you the kind of person he was. He'd park it in the grass like that to make sure he wasn't taking a space away from a customer, even when he barely had any customers left. That's why it's still out there where he left it."

"Am I to understand no one's looked at it yet?"

"No mechanics, if that's what you mean. For about a year I went out every few days and got the engine going. I was religious about it. Then I got lazy and stopped, and when I went to start it up again, the engine was dead. I'm not very mechanical, I'm afraid."

"I'm a sucker for fins," Larry says, nodding at the Ranchero's. "Fins and those single headlamps. What perfect aesthetic touches. If you ever doubted that Ford's designers were artists, there's your proof right there. For some reason the double headlamps never did it for me."

"Is this really going to be free except for parts? Is that true?"

"Yes, it is, Nico."

43

"But how can you do that? You charge a lot extra for parts, is that how?"

"No," Cornell says, looking offended. "That wouldn't be right."

"But how do you make money?"

"We don't," Larry says, gazing off at a pair of buzzards circling in the sky. "We do this because it brings meaning to our lives." He smiles at Nico now. "Can't tell you how good it makes us feel every time we save another one."

Nico covers his face with his hands. He might be crying. "That is . . . well, it's unbelievable. Thank you, thank you so much. I didn't know there were people like the three of you still left in this mean old world."

The three of us. That's what he said.

He shoulders the door back open. "I'll come check on you later," he says. "Or, better yet, come inside when you're ready. Breakfast is on me today."

Larry and Cornell walk over to the edge of the parking lot and stand side by side, shoulders nearly touching. It's hard to know what they make of the Ranchero. Their eyes squeeze tight, and so do their lips.

"Sorry you had to go through that," Cornell whispers.

I need a minute to figure out that he's talking to the Ranchero.

In his notebook Larry does a quick sketch of the scene. An odd-looking little pickup sits in a field. A couple of birds circle in the sky—not buzzards but jays, big fat ones. Off to one side is a road. Off to the other is a diner with letters on the roof. Each letter is a tall wooden cutout. In Larry's drawing the letters are all there—the O hasn't fallen off yet—and they're all straight.

"June," Cornell says. "There's a Weedwacker in the back of the truck. There on your left as you walk in. Go get it, please. And grab me some protective eyewear while you're at it, will you?"

"What is protective eyewear?"

"Goggles. You'll see a bunch on the shelves, middle right."

The doors to the back squeak a little when I pull them open, and I nearly fall over at the sight of all that's in there. All along I was thinking the container held only "tools and what-not," as Cornell said, but it's more like a combination Home Depot and auto-parts store, with everything neatly arranged.

I see rubber belts and hoses and metal objects whose names and functions I couldn't tell you. There are hubcaps, windshields and windows, a fender, bumpers, and doors. Way in back, hanging on the wall, there's a small sign that says GOD FORD. The board is a three-foot-long white plank with blue letters. I look at the sign more closely and notice one more thing: The shadow of a heart holds the space between the words, so the sign actually says GOD LOVES FORD.

I see a bunch of other stuff: water jugs and bottles and cans of assorted oils, cleaners, and degreasers, a cardboard box holding bags of sunflower seeds, at least a dozen toolboxes,

45

and a couple of Igloos stacked against a wall. The cooler on the bottom is as big as a coffin, and it has TIME INSENSITIVE written in permanent marker on the side. The other one has TIME SENSITIVE spelled out on the lid.

Rearview and side mirrors hang from wires overhead and reflect the light as they twist this way and that. They bump against one another and make a musical tinkling sound like wind chimes. It isn't until I catch a glimpse of myself in one of them that my chest caves and I turn away.

I carry the goggles and Weedwacker out to Cornell. He takes his time with the goggles, making sure they fit just right on his face, then he starts pulling the string coiled up in the Weedwacker's motor. The motor starts, and Cornell walks out in the grass and knocks the biggest clumps down. Bit by bit the Ranchero is revealed. The front half resembles a car, but there's a long open box in the back half where the back seat and trunk should be. They made some interesting things to ride around in in the old days. This one is painted black.

Cornell still has the grass along one side to chop down, but he stops and signals to me. He hands me the goggles and the Weedwacker. "Your turn," he says.

"But is it . . . ? I mean, I never—"

"Nothing to it, June. You hold it with both hands here at your side"—he's demonstrating now—"the right one down here, the left one here on this deal here. And you carefully swing it from one side to the other. That little button there is for the gas. Goose it and the rotation of your line speeds up. You want to take it slow. No hurry, all right? Here's the kill switch if you wrap around something and need to power off. Okay, we always start with the eyewear. Put them on and make sure they fit nice and snug. Today we're just clearing an area. No fancy landscaping moves, you understand? I'm here if you need me."

I'm not saying it's the most fun I ever had, but I really do enjoy myself. Everybody seems to have a natural talent at something, and mine might be whacking weeds. Weeds don't stand a chance with June Ball going at them.

When I finish, Cornell looks over at Larry and says, "Got ourselves a Weedwacker genius."

I pull the goggles off. They come over and take turns slapping my shoulders.

Now that we've carved out a clearing, Cornell drives the truck into the field and parks next to the Ranchero. He climbs into the container and attaches a coiled hose to the side of a machine that I'd barely noticed until now. "This is a combination air compressor and generator," he says. "A generator generates energy. It's your power source. We're going to be inflating the tires. The compressor will do that—it's your air source. This unit will also power your tools and your lights and fans. Cousin Larry's also got it rigged with a charging station for his phone. Incredible, huh? That's right. All he has to do is plug it in."

He gets the generator and compressor started and then

hops down, holding the end of the hose. "See how easy?" he says, and blows some air at my face. "Nothing to it."

He does the first of the tires and uses a little pen-size stick to check the pressure. Then he has me do the other ones, crouching next to me to make sure I'm doing it right. You squeeze this flat deal shaped like a tongue and the air blows out. You have to be careful because it comes out hard.

"Looks like we have a genius for tires, too," he says when I'm done.

Next it's Larry's turn to teach me something. He replaces the old battery in the Ranchero with a new one. He shows me the different terminals, the positive and the negative, the red and the black, and explains why you don't want to confuse them. Next he takes a five-gallon can full of gas and pours it into the Ranchero's fuel tank.

"There was no gas because it evaporated," he says. "Fuel pump went dry—come see, son. That white stuff there? That's oxidation. But I'll pour a sip of gas in the carburetor, and that should wake it up. My eyebrows caught fire doing this once, so just to be safe you'd better stand back a ways. Just a few more feet—one more, one more. There you go."

Five minutes later and they get it started. There's a muffled explosion and then bullets of smoke shoot from the tailpipe. The Ranchero sounds raggedy at first but evens out once Larry fools around with the engine. Then I start hearing another sound. It's coming from behind us. I wheel around, and Nico's standing over by the delivery door. He's clapping his hands so hard you know they've got to sting.

"Bravo!" he calls out. "Bravo!"

Larry and Cornell give him little waves to show that they appreciate being appreciated. Nico points at me, and I give in and give him one, too. I feel a little weird doing that—it was Larry and Cornell who did the real work. But now all three of them are nodding and smiling at me, showing that I earned it.

"Feels good, doesn't it?" Larry says.

"Yes, sir."

"That's what it's all about. That right there."

Nico says he has to finish cooking our breakfast. Once he goes back inside, Cornell says, "Most jobs we'll be doing this summer won't be as easy as this one, June. Nico could've made the repairs himself. I wouldn't want to embarrass him by announcing that, but he really didn't need us—not to fix his Ford, anyway." He pauses and looks back at the diner. "We'll wash it and take it for a test drive later on, but what do you say we try those pancakes first. You hungry, son?"

He starts walking toward the front of the building even before I answer, and then Larry runs out ahead of him.

Cornell says, "Whoa there," and takes off trying to catch him. They're racing now to see who can reach the diner first. What they don't know is that I'm fast for a big kid, and suddenly all three of us are hightailing it across the lot. Daddy taught me that by using your arms and legs as pistons you can generate speed, and I should credit him for that because it proves to be the difference. Maybe they're just being nice again, but I don't think so. As I move out ahead they start yelling behind me, "No . . . wait . . . come on . . . June, hey, June . . ." Then Cornell reaches out and grabs at my jersey. I feel a tug, but I can see the end zone all of a sudden and there's no stopping me.

The little cowbell on the door handle jingles to signal my victory.

EIGHT

THREE PLATES ARE WAITING FOR US on the counter, each one piled high with pancakes. Larry and Cornell wait until I choose the middle stool before sitting on either side of me. We really should wash our hands, but that might disappoint our host, considering he's already served the food.

I've seen a lot of pancakes in my day but never any more beautiful. Each one is fluffy and the perfect golden-brown color. They put microwave and box-mix pancakes to shame. They make Mama's look like the work of a rank amateur. If pancakes ever can be considered works of art, these would have to be the ones. I'm not exaggerating when I tell you they belong in a museum.

"Sorry it's so dark in here," Nico says. "You need more light, just tell me. I can move you closer to the windows."

"It's fine," Larry says. "A lovely ambience, in fact."

I might agree with him if I knew what an ambience is. The counter lamps really could be brighter, and the rest of the place is so dark it reminds me of a funeral home. I'm thinking I should ask Nico for a flashlight, but something stops me. It might be his feelings.

"Has anybody noticed the price of light bulbs lately?" Cornell says. "Ridiculous."

"Not only bulbs," Larry says. "The electricity to fire them. Oh, don't get me started on the power company."

Nico's only other customer is still sitting at the far end of the counter. His forehead is resting on the Formica. We're all looking at him when Nico says, "That's Ray. He was Grandpa's friend. He comes here to sleep. He says it's quieter than at his house. I know it's rude that he puts his head like that—I wish his hair wouldn't fall in the syrup—but I'm grateful for the company." Nico starts wiping the area by our plates, his wet towel soaking up the spills.

"I'm afraid to ask," he says, "but did the Ranchero need any new parts?" He reaches into his shirt pocket and fishes out a few wrinkled bills.

Larry and Cornell both shake their heads. "No, it didn't," Cornell says. "But we're the ones who should be offering to pay you, Nico. A Ranchero. Wow. I mean, my heavens. What a privilege."

"But you changed out the battery and added gas—I saw that much, I was watching from around back."

"Oh, we already had those, leftovers from another job. Please, don't even think about it."

Nico lets out a sigh and slides the money back in his

pocket. "Grandpa should've built closer to the interstate. He had the opportunity, fifty years ago, but he wanted to be here for the town. He kept thinking it would grow out more this way, and he didn't want to leave. The sad part is that the town left him. Nobody wants to live around here anymore, not since the forge closed. Drive up the road a few miles and get yourself an eyeful."

"Nico, your pancakes belong in the Pancake Hall of Fame," I say. And I mean it. I could weep I am so filled with emotion at how delicious they are.

"Thank you, June. Thanks a lot. But I can't take the credit. It was all Grandpa, the great Oscar Alejandro. I learned from the master."

The whole time we're talking Larry is staring at the ceiling. His lips move as he seems to be counting the light cans and fixtures. Nico starts taking the plates away, and Larry stands and excuses himself. "Back in a few," he says. I figure he needs the facilities, but instead he goes to the door and steps outside.

We can see him through the windows. He's standing in the middle of the lot now, and he's looking up at the roof and counting again.

When he's done he walks over to the truck and removes some things from the back—a bucket, sponges, a bottle of blue liquid, a spring hose, a broom, towels, my travel bag. Then he climbs in the cab and roars off.

"Why don't we take the Ranchero for a test drive," Cornell

tells me. "Check the brakes and steering and everything. But first I thought we should wash it. You ever wash your daddy's pickup?"

"No, sir. Never did. He never washes it, either. I heard him tell Mama once that is why God made the rain."

"The rain, huh? To wash his pickup?"

"Yes, sir."

"Your dad always cracked me up. You know something, June? I'm seeing him in you—the best of him. Nobody finer than Henry Ball, I guarantee you that. Oh, I know he's had his struggles in recent years, but that is bound to turn. And when it does we're going to be there for him. We love him, too, June. And we miss him, too. It's the bighearted ones who have the problems. The sensitive ones. The ones who are made right and who care. Larry and I would do anything for cousin Henry. That's one reason you're with us now—to show we have his back, after all the years he was off fighting and had ours."

There's a lot to say, if only I could say it. He just knocked the air out of my lungs. "Thank you," I manage somehow.

"For what?" he says.

I follow him outside and he gets in the Ranchero and drives it around to the pile Larry made. He grabs the broom and hands it to me and tells me to sweep out the bed. Start at the bulkhead and work toward the tailgate. Get all the crud out. Then we can wash it good, make it pretty again.

"Now here's what you need to know about washing a

car," he says, as he's screwing the spring hose into a faucet on the side of the building. "You always want to start at your highest point and work down. That way you're telling the dirt where it needs to go. If you work from the bottom up, what happens?"

I'm trying to see it, but I can't.

"You're just dirtying what you already cleaned, right? That's all you're doing. You're making things hard for yourself."

Most kids wouldn't like being bossed around, but I'm fine with it. At least my mind and my body are occupied. Back home, right now all I'd be doing is tearing the house apart looking for where Mama hid her chocolate-covered raisins.

I've handled a broom plenty of times in my day, so it's no big deal to sweep out the bed. As soon as I finish I get the hose and turn the water on and start the rinsing. The top's too tall for me to reach from the ground, so I step back up in the bed and get to the roof that way. It's hard to keep from getting wet, and I'm soaked before long. As I work, Cornell stands in the field watching and stroking his whiskers. Even when I'm applying the soap with a sponge he doesn't help. I'm building a case against him all the way until I finish and he says, "Man, what a talent. Good lord, June. And this was your first time?"

"Yes, sir."

"Hard for me to believe that."

I can feel the blood come up in my face. It's a good kind of blood. I grab a towel and start drying off the hood. I wish I could make it look better. The paint has little shine left, even in the sunlight. When I'm done Cornell picks up a second towel and dries my hair with it the way you'd dry a dog after a bath, rubbing so hard my scalp hurts and my hair sticks straight up. "Go on and change into some dry clothes, why don't you?" he says. He gives my bag a nudge with the toe of his boot. "Wouldn't want you to catch cold, now, would we?"

"A cold is a virus," I say. "You don't catch it from wet clothes. You catch it from people who are infected with it."

"Listen to you, Dr. Ball," Cornell says.

"It's true."

"Either way, you need to put on dry clothes. I won't be looking." He turns his back to me as if that is enough.

"But people'll be able to see me—from the road. I can't do it out here."

"What people?"

I look around. He's right about there being no people. "What about Ray and Nico? They don't count?"

"No. No, they don't. One's sleeping, and the other's busy. Go hide behind the Ranchero if you're going to be all shy about it."

I don't like anybody looking at me naked. Never did. I don't have the best body, but it's more than that. I must've been born modest. From when I first heard the story about Adam and Eve I've been grateful to them for eating the apple. Can you imagine a world where everybody walked around without any clothes on? It would be hard to eat in restaurants. You couldn't do it.

I stand behind the Ranchero and change in a hurry. I just hate having to swap out my Aaron Rodgers jersey. We've been through a lot together, number twelve and me. I replace it with a pocket tee.

When I'm done I walk back to the diner with Cornell. Nico's waiting for us outside on a bench. He moves over to the end to let us know he wants us to sit with him, but Cornell has other plans. "Thought we should take the Ranchero for that test drive before Larry gets back and we head out," he says.

"Leaving already?" Nico says. "But you just got here."

Cornell shrugs. "I know, I'm sorry. It's always harder to leave a place than to get to it, even when we have to drive a thousand miles."

"Could you just sit for a while?" Nico says. "Ray doesn't say a lot, and I can't tell you how much I've enjoyed having someone to talk to."

Cornell looks at him. "Okay, Nico. We're here for you, brother." He sits at the other end, and I sit in the middle.

It turns out Nico was in his first year of trade school when Grandpa died. He'd wanted to be an X-ray tech, but suddenly he had the diner to run. His mom and dad were still alive, but they'd divorced years ago and now lived in other states with their new partners.

"I never felt like we were a family," Nico says. "Not really. It was more like I was a mistake they wanted to forget. Thank God for Grandpa. He took me in and raised me from first grade—I grew up in Oscar's. Did you notice that room attached to the back of the building? That was our house; it's still my house. When Grandpa got sick, he asked me to keep the store going—he called the diner a store. It was his dream and his dying wish. I didn't want to let him down, so here I am."

"You can always go back to school," Cornell says.

"I could, sure, but Oscar's would have to close. Grandpa made me promise I'd never do that."

Cornell removes a bag of sunflower seeds from his pocket and offers it to Nico and me. We shake our heads, and he opens his mouth and slides some in. He manipulates the seeds with his tongue and a finger until they form a chaw that protrudes from the side of his mouth.

We stare off at the road. Cars pass by, but nobody turns in.

"It's not always this slow," Nico says. He looks at his hands. "Well, that's not true."

"I wouldn't take it personally," Cornell says. "You have an excellent product in those pancakes. They are like eiderdown in the mouth. But you can't expect to serve them if there's no one left in the area to serve them to."

Nico removes an order pad and a pencil from his apron pocket. "I'm writing that down," he says.

"Please don't take this as a criticism of Grandpa, Nico, but should we impose our dreams on others, especially those

58

who love us and would do most anything to please us? Cousin Larry and I meet Ford owners all the time who inherit vehicles they have no use for. They hang on to them because others asked them to and those others are gone."

Nico finishes writing and puts his pen and pad away. "I miss Grandpa more than anything, but sometimes I wish he hadn't loved me so much."

NINE

THE FIRST ONES ARRIVE before we can take the Ranchero for a spin. They're an elderly couple who say they met Larry at a gas station up the road. They saw the antique box truck and asked about it, and by and by, quite unexpectedly, the subject of pancakes came up.

They move past us and sit at the counter.

Right behind them is a family of five tired of the same old bacon and eggs every day. Not ten minutes ago, a bald-headed man with a long beard commented on the beauty of their Econoline van, and then he asked them if they'd heard about a diner called Oscar's.

These come next: a minister with some time to burn before choir practice, a farmer's wife tired of her own cooking, and a lineman who came down from his pole to discuss cost-efficient LED bulbs with Larry.

Nico looks nervous as everyone files in.

"Nothing to it," Cornell says. "I'll help you with the cooking. June, you work the counter and take the orders."

"But how do I do that?"

"You ask them what they want. Simple as that. Then you tell Nico and me, and we get it ready."

It turns out anybody could do it, especially at a place where every order is for pancakes. As they're cooking on the grill, Larry comes in carrying bags full of light bulbs. All the diners greet him—you'd think they were lifelong friends—and the preacher starts singing a hymn with words he makes up on the spot, all of them having to do with flapjacks.

"Order up," Cornell calls out from the kitchen window.

"Order *up*," he calls again, when I'm not distributing the plates fast enough.

Larry finds a stepladder in a storeroom and uses it to reach the cans in the ceiling, and one after another he changes the bulbs. The diners are so busy eating they don't seem to mind the dust that keeps raining down. When he finishes he flips a wall switch and the restaurant hums with light.

"Hallelujah!" the minister calls out.

Nico comes out for a look and there's wild applause because he cooked the pancakes. He seems to want to cry again. Cornell stands off to the side where no one can see him, making sure the right person gets the credit.

Larry claps Nico's back with his hand, and Nico's knees buckle a little.

"I'm grateful, Mr. Larry, but I can't . . ." He is struggling to come up with the right word to finish his sentence. "*This*," he finally says, and grabs at the air, which I take to mean the light.

"The bulbs were in the truck," Larry says.

"Not until you bought them and put them there. And that was just a little while ago." Some clear stuff is draining from his nostrils.

"If you're going to do something, Nico, do it all out, a hundred miles an hour. It's fine to fail, as long as you try, but it's not fine if you're standing around in the dark watching your grandpa's friend sleep with his head on the counter."

Another customer walks in. She wonders if she could have a cup of coffee to go. Two sugars, no cream. "Coming right up," I tell her.

I've already found where Nico keeps the Styrofoam cups and lids. Same for the straws and napkins and spoons. A little box holds the sugar packets. *Come on, dude. You can do this.*

"We used to come here when I was little," the customer says. "I'd forgotten how pretty it is."

The youngest members of the Econoline family are playing hide-and-seek under the tables. In the new hymn he's singing, the minister asks for his check.

I'm busy with my chores, but I do notice when Larry moves outside to the truck and takes the extension ladder from the back. And I can hear him when he gets up on the roof and starts thumping around.

"Well, since I'm already here, how about some of what they just had?" says the customer who wanted the coffee. She points to the empty plates on the counter. They all held pancakes until a few minutes ago.

"Order up," Cornell calls out from the kitchen.

I hope you'll forgive me for bringing up my dad all the time. It's hard for me to get him out of my head.

Whenever I see something new, like what just happened at Oscar's, I can't help but wish he was seeing it with me. When he was having a good day, there never was a subject I could ask him about and he didn't have an answer, even when the answer was "I don't know, June, but give me some time and I'll find out for you."

Today I'd have to ask him about Larry and Cornell. "I know they're supposed to be Ford men," I'd say, "but they're really more than that, aren't they?"

Things in Oscar's finally settle down, and Cornell and I take off on that test drive. We go up to where the town starts, then he turns in front of a vacant store and drives back. We don't say anything because he's concentrating, listening for sounds that would indicate problems.

"Grandpa babied it, for sure," Cornell says as we're turning into the diner's lot. "You can feel how happy the Ranchero is, can't you, June? I love it when they're like that."

Larry's still on the roof, the extension ladder stretching

from the parking lot to the gutter. He's restored the O to where it belongs, he's straightened out the other letters, and he's given them all a quick paint job.

Before we leave, Cornell has a few more words for Nico. The rush is over and we're outside on the bench, cooling off. "It's your life, Nico, nobody else's. Let us hear from you if the Ranchero needs more work. It looks good parked in front of the diner, but I'm sure they'd admire it just as much at the trade school."

An SUV is pulling in from the road. It seems tentative at first, as if the driver is trying to decide if he has the right place. As it gets closer, I can see the blue oval on the front grill.

"Best pancakes anywhere," Larry says. "You should start a website and run some pictures. Show what a friendly place you have here. And brag about yourself. I know that might be hard to do—you impress me as a humble young man. But let everyone know how neat you are. It's called advertising. Why be good at something if you're keeping it secret from the world?"

With all the lights on in the diner, you can see everything inside through the windows, including Ray, who's just now waking up. The brightness from all the new bulbs seems to startle him. Sitting up on his stool, he looks around as if for something he lost.

Nico hurries back inside.

The SUV is full of kids who just left softball practice.

TEN

NO SIGNIFICANT OTHERS OR KIDS, and they haven't mentioned pets, either. But after our time at Oscar's, I'm starting to see why it might be enough for Larry and Cornell to have only Ford in their lives.

Cornell is behind the wheel now, giving Larry a chance to finish the drawing in his notebook. He adds little marks around the bulbs poking out from the lamps, and when you see these marks you know the lights are on and you're welcome inside. He puts a bunch of cars in the parking lot and on the road, some of them with kids and dogs hanging out of the windows. He makes all the cars Fords, but I don't question him about that detail, understanding by now that he can't help it. Next he draws more birds that aren't buzzards, and a sun with giant rays, and grass in the fields more like what you see on a putting green at a golf course. To show that he's done, he signs the drawing in the lower-right corner, putting his initials only and the date.

He opens the glove compartment and stuffs the notebook inside. It's one of dozens stored there.

"I noticed something," I say. "When you first started the drawing, you already had the Ranchero looking good. That was even before the repairs."

"Right."

"And why is that?"

He settles back in the seat, letting himself relax. "Ever take a personality test, June? No? Well, I did once, long time ago. Found out I'm an optimist and a dreamer and a goal setter. I see the world as I'd like it to be, then I go out and try to make it that way. Answer your question? Nobody wants their picture made on their worst day, not even a Ranchero."

Along with the notebooks, I see a map in the glove compartment. It's old and wrinkly and folded in the shape of an accordion, and there's a Gulf Oil stamp on the cover. Larry takes it out and opens it, and I see little blue stars stretching from one coast to the other and from Canada clear down to Mexico.

Go outside tonight and look at the sky. That's how many stars there are on that map.

"Are these all the places where you've worked on Fords?" I say. "You really went to Orlando? Disney's in Orlando."

"Went there several times," Cornell says. "They got themselves a lot of Fords in the state of Florida."

Larry points to where we are now, which is just a little to the west of where Oscar's would be. "We do the map for kicks. It gives us a sense of accomplishment to see all the stars. I can remember the first star we ever did, way back when we started. It was before we had the cell phone and GPS, and it was here, right here next to Sheboygan Falls, in Kohler." He reaches back into the glove box and digs out a pen. "I was hoping you'd do the honors and add a new star," he says.

When I hesitate he only pushes it closer.

"Go ahead. Add a star for the Ranchero—here, June, right here."

I never could draw very well, and it's even harder with the truck jostling me every time we hit a bump. When I finish, my star is double the size of all the others. I shouldn't have kept trying to make it perfect. That only made me make it bigger. I finish, and Larry says, "I wonder if Nico could feel scratching just now on the top of his head, when you were coloring the star." He is smiling. "Ford blue always completes the story."

The air rushing in throws their beards up over their shoulders. Every now and then a gust blows the hair in my face. It's like getting slapped by a couple of mops. I close my eyes and take it for as long as I can.

"You boys need a trim," I say.

Each one rubs his bald head with his hand. "We sure do, don't we?" Cornell says, and snorts a laugh. "Hey, cousin, told you he was just like Henry."

"He is! He is!" Larry says.

"I was talking about your beards. I've been taking a beating."

"Oh." And they tuck their whiskers into their coveralls.

The radio's been playing old farts like Nat King Cole and Frank Sinatra, and Larry's been working on the schedule. He does this by switching back and forth from text and voice mail messages to plugging data into the day planner in his phone. He types in names, addresses, and the various Fords that need attention. From the information an owner sends him, he's able to calculate how long a job will take.

"Don't despair, Mrs. McBean," he tells one lady. "The cavalry's on its way. Be there as soon as we can."

We're on the interstate now, heading south on a path parallel with the Mississippi River. I know this because I can see us on the map on Larry's phone. *Would you mind terribly if we borrow your field?* Larry writes in a text. He gets a thumbs-up in reply. *Eternally grateful, wo de pengyou.*

"*Wo de pengyou* is Chinese for 'my friend,'" he says.

Cornell is so focused behind the wheel he rarely even blinks, although he does keep announcing the names of cars that pass us by in the opposite lanes. He somehow knows what they are even from a distance, and for the longest time I can't figure out how he does it: "Mazda ... Mercedes ... Honda ... Toyota ... Chevy, bah! Bah, Chevy! ... Dodge ... Volvo ... Chrysler ... Mitsubishi ... Oh, Tesla! ..."

It's only when he sees a Ford that he gets really excited. He pumps the horn and yells, "Ford! *Ford!* Hey, look, a Ford!"

"The logos," Larry explains after Cornell quiets down. "See

them on the grills, June? Some people call them emblems or badges—both are fine—but we prefer logos, don't we, Cornell?"

"Right. Logos. Ford! *Ford!* Hey, look, a Ford!"

"Every manufacturer has one," Larry says. "Get to recognize them at a glance, and you'll be able to keep up with your cousin."

It's not that hard, really. I start matching what Cornell says with the cars that shoot past us, and before long I'm yelling out names. My eyesight must be better than his, because I'm identifying the logos before he does.

"Ford! *Ford!* Hey, look, a Ford!" I shout.

Cornell pumps the horn as a shiny little Escort slides by, but I can tell he was having more fun before I got in on the act.

Larry starts drawing again, this time a road full of cars with their front grills in sharp focus. "June, this is a hard thing to talk about, but it must be done."

"If it's about girls I already know everything."

"No, son, if only it were that simple. I'm not a prejudiced person, but what we haven't talked about are the bow ties among us."

"Ties? *Bow* ties? Yeah, I agree, dumbest things ever."

Larry's drawing a pickup with a Chevy logo on front, and it's unlike any of the Fords I've seen him draw. It's a disaster, in other words, that just crashed into a ditch. Steam pours from the engine, and the fenders hang to the ground. Big, fat buzzards roost on the roof, and their droppings run down the windshield. The car's owner is sitting under a tree with his face in his hands. His glasses are on the ground next to him, and it looks like the buzzards bombed them, too.

"By bow tie I mean the other side," he says. "You might even say the *dark* side. Bow ties are Chevy people. They are some sick individuals, my friend."

"And Chevy people wear bow ties?"

"No. They don't have the *class* to wear bow ties. It's their logo. You haven't noticed what it's shaped like?" He points to the drawing and starts to get hysterical. "Look. That's a bow tie. That is definitely a bow tie."

I've seen plenty of them on the road today, but until now the logo didn't register with me as a tie. I just thought it was a pretty decoration.

"Come on, cousin," Cornell says. "We all have to get along in this world. Love and respect one another. Good Lord made us all different for a reason. If we were all the same, that wouldn't be very interesting, now, would it?"

We drive on, and Cornell starts announcing the cars again. I keep quiet and let him do it by himself. He only whispers when it's a Chevy, I suppose to keep Larry from melting down any more than he already has.

In his drawing of the wrecked Chevy, Larry adds the word *LOSER* to the front of the guy's shirt, then he puts his initials in the corner.

We exit onto another small road that leads into the country. "We have a friend, Dr. Chen," Cornell says. "He owns some property where we like to camp when we're in the area. It's a wildflower preserve. A hundred acres. As pretty a patch as you'll ever see."

"And it's wildflowers? I thought preserves were for animals."

"Dr. Chen is a plant biologist. When he's not out on his land cultivating poppies and milkmaids and knapweed, he's lecturing about them at the university in Urbana–Champaign. He's a professor there."

We turn onto a dirt lane and drive over a cattleguard into a huge field. Cornell stops, and all three of us get out. The day is ending, and what remains of the sunlight pours out over an endless blanket of color. I see patches of lavender and yellow and crimson and white, all swimming in the breeze. Hummingbirds whiz by, and butterflies as big as your hand move from one flower to the next. It's so beautiful I wonder if it's even real.

"Better get busy before it gets dark," Larry says. He opens the back, and he and Cornell hop inside, then together they drag out a large bag made of the same material as my travel bag. They pull it over to a spot next to the lane, and Larry holds one end while Cornell pulls the bag's contents out of the other. It's a tent, a big one. They start putting it up, moving like a dance team that's done this number a few times before. As we're lifting the heavy canvas on wooden poles, I catch a scent of bleach mixed with old socks.

Not so nice, if you really want to know.

The tent can hold up to eight adults. There are double flaps for the door, and Cornell pulls them open and ties them off. Then he and Larry arrange pallets made of army blankets on the floor. These are our beds, spaced out a few feet apart. On top of each one Cornell drops a sponge pillow and a sheet. They reek, too, but more of mildew than socks and bleach.

"June, you're our guest so you get to choose the bed you want," Larry says. "I'd recommend staying as far away from cousin Cornell as possible. The boy has digestive issues and is prone to letting loose just as you're about to nod off."

I look over at Cornell. "Is that true?"

"No, not all the time it isn't."

"I don't mind the middle," I say. "Fastest way out the door."

"In case of explosions," Larry says.

Cornell's face is burning red. "Will you stop scaring the boy?"

"*Ka-pow!*" Larry says, as if a car just backfired.

They arrange their clothes next. Each one makes a neat pile of his spare coveralls, undershirts, socks, and boxer shorts. When that's done they arrange their toiletries on the floor. They're pretty much the same things Daddy keeps in his medicine cabinet at home: deodorant sticks, toothpaste, dental floss, foot powder, jock-itch ointment. They also have hair-brushes, which makes me wonder why until I remember that their beards are made of hair.

Compared to their piles, mine is modest. Tell you the

truth, I don't have a pile. Instead it's just some things scattered on the floor where my feet will be.

"I need the bathroom," I say.

"Which one?" Larry asks.

"I don't want to have to say. It's private."

He and Cornell are setting up a Coleman cookstove near the entrance to the tent. "We won't be here long, June, so we didn't plan on digging a privy." Cornell points to a little tree over by the cattleguard. "Why don't you go behind that one?"

"Too close to the road," I say. "And too skinny."

"Then that one. The old oak. What do you think?" He's pointing to a big tree off in the distance, way in the middle of the wildflowers. "You need toilet paper?"

"If I say yes, then you'll know which one I need to do."

"I'll get you some," Larry says. And he goes for a roll in the truck.

"I'm sorry," I say after he hands it to me, and I start walking.

"Sorry? What the heck for? For being a human being?" He actually pronounces it *bean*. "Don't ever apologize for that, you hear? That paper is biodegradable, by the way. It's not a problem to leave it."

I hate to trudge through the flowers. I hate to kill any, but I really have no choice. And it's getting to where I can't wait much longer. "Sorry," I say to some little yellow ones. "Sorry, terribly sorry."

The whole time I'm looking around for snakes. I hate

snakes. I arrive at the tree and stand there a minute trying to decide how best to do it. There's a worm and a water bug on the ground at my feet. I feel like apologizing to them, too. It doesn't seem fair that their territory is being invaded this way. They must be wondering what the heck is going on, why this kid they don't know is leaning back against the trunk of their favorite tree.

"Cover your eyes," I say.

It is not easy, doing that. In fact, it is very difficult and requires a lot of effort, especially when it's time for the toilet paper. I keep wondering what Dr. Chen will think next time he visits his wildflowers and walks over to see how his oak tree is doing. I hope the worm and the water bug make it.

I finish and walk back to the campsite. I put the roll in the truck, then wash my hands with some liquid soap and a bottle of water.

"What was that word again?" I say. "Bio what?"

"Biodegradable. That means it degrades naturally over time and doesn't hang around littering the earth. Little invisible bugs eat it. Microorganisms. A good, hard rain and there'll be nothing left."

You're probably thinking I've stooped pretty low, doing it out there. But is that my fault? I might not be a human bean, but I'm definitely a human being.

Yet one more thing to be mad at Daddy about.

If I were home now, I could play *Madden* and have a peek at one of those channels Mama warned me about, one she was supposed to have blocked. Even better, I could watch reunion videos and wonder about the parents who care enough to return home, when mine is still on the lam.

"June, the Time Sensitive cooler," Cornell says. "Think you could help me carry it down from the back?"

At the truck, I grab a handle and strain against the weight, but the whole time I'm seeing Dr. Chen having a heart attack under his oak tree.

ELEVEN

THEY DRIVE A POLE IN THE GROUND, then hang a gas lantern from it. Cornell lights the lantern with a match, and it hisses like baby insects and gives off a yellow-green glow. Next they pull out some chairs and arrange them in a semi-circle in front of the cookstove. Two of them are director's chairs, with one that has *Artist* and the other *Studio Assistant* in white paint across the backs. The one they get for me is called a Campeche chair, which I've never heard of until I'm actually sitting in it. The frame is made of bent wood, and the seat and back are leather. Some Ford owner in New Mexico, a lady with an adobe house, gave it to them in gratitude for saving her vintage something or other.

Cornell opens the lid to the cooler. I see crushed ice covering vegetables like lettuce and celery and bell peppers. There are also packs of steaks and pork chops and cartons of butter and milk and whipping cream. And cheese. Yeah, lots and lots of cheese.

"How often do you stop to fill that thing?" I ask.

"Three times a week, maybe," Larry answers. "When it's getting close to empty."

"But where?"

"Well, wherever we happen to be. We find the nearest grocery store and load up. It's not complicated, June."

"But the ice must melt."

"Yeah, it melts. Sure. But we just drain the water out when it's time and buy more ice, usually when we stop to get gas for the truck. We're always on the lookout for stations with ice machines."

"Why don't you just go through the drive-through at McDonald's when you're hungry?"

"Truck's too big," Larry says, "and Cornell cooks better. I might be biased because we're related, but the man has a gift."

Cornell slips on an apron that says *ALEXA, PLAY ME SOME DISCO* across the front, then he removes a pack of steaks from the cooler. This one holds three rib eyes. He tears the plastic wrapping away, then seasons the meat with black pepper and sea salt and lays the steaks on a skillet that's been heating up on the stove. The skillet is one of those old-time cast-iron jobs, and it's big enough to cover two burners. As the steaks sizzle and darken against the heat, Cornell opens a can of baked beans and plops them into a dented pot with a broken handle. He sprinkles the beans with garlic and onion powder and places them over a flame.

While all this is going on, Larry is making a salad. He slices tomatoes and shreds a head of lettuce, then he carves small chunks from a fist-size block of mozzarella cheese. Everything goes into a mixing bowl. Before adding the dressing, he takes a piece of the cheese in his fingers and holds it out to me.

"None for me, thank you," I tell him.

"But you love cheese."

It's true, there's nothing better, but I keep flashing to the worm and the water bug. "Just not hungry at the moment," I say.

He flicks the cheese into his mouth and stares at me as he chews. "Not a problem, June. What do you say we call your mom and tell her about your day?"

"Can we wait until tomorrow?"

"Sure. We can wait. But I was looking forward to telling her how well you're doing. I know it must be hard, being out on the road with two virtual strangers. But before long it'll be you who makes the salad. After that, you'll be cooking the steaks. Same with the Fords. You might just be our head weed whacker and car washer for now, but the day is coming when you'll be changing the oil and patching the flats."

He seems to remember something, and he walks over and disappears into the back of the truck. When he returns he's carrying a bucket with a car part sticking out. "Ever see one of these?" He answers before I can take a guess. "It's a carburetor. New cars don't have them because everything now is fuel injection, but this summer there'll be a carburetor in most of the Fords we see. The carburetor, this thing here, is a device in internal combustion engines that takes in air and mixes it with a fine spray of gas, creating a combustion mixture. The carburetor's responsible for power and speed, so it's a crucial part of the engine. The one we have here is a Holley 750. It's made for high-performance cars, hot rods mainly. Today we're going to take it apart, piece by piece, then we're going to put it back together again."

"I can't . . . I mean . . . *We? How?*"

"Well, with a screwdriver. Let's start with that." And he hands me one. "Okay, get after it, June."

There's a flap or a valve or something in the middle, and there's a screw next to it. I decide to begin with the screw, but I can't even crack it. The screwdriver won't stay in the little slot where you're supposed to put the tip. The tip? I'm sure there's another name for it. Nobody ever told me.

"Here," Larry says. "Better yet, just watch me."

In seconds he has the screw out. "This is your accelerator pump squirt . . . Top thing here is your choke . . . Oh, right, the needle and seat assembly, here . . . And your fuel line . . . Oh, and this is your float bowl in your storage area for your fuel . . . on a Holley there are two . . . And your metering plate . . . again, not all carburetors have them but a Holley does . . . And on the plate there's a power valve . . . see it? *June?* Hey, son, wake up. Do you see the power valve . . . ?"

"Dinner's ready," Cornell calls out.

Larry dumps the carburetor parts in the bucket and scrambles past me to get to the food.

I will give him this much: At least he's got his priorities straight.

That steak was smaller than I usually like but I can't remember ever eating a tastier one, even the times Daddy used to grill on Sundays after Packers games. When we finish, Larry puts the carburetor back together, then takes it apart again.

"Like a Rubik's cube," I tell him. "I'll never be able to do that."

"But you will, June. You might not believe it yet, but you have it in you to be great. You'll beat me at the carburetor"— he is whispering now—"just as you beat cousin Cornell naming cars out on the interstate."

We clean up the dirty pans and dishes in tubs full of soapy water, then we sit in our chairs. Cornell takes the radio from the truck and leans it back against a bowl on the camp table. He finds a station playing piano music, and we listen while the stars and the moon shine down on us. I hear a familiar hum, and Larry fumbles to get his phone out of his pocket. He glances at the screen.

"Ah," he says, and taps the green dot.

Mama's booming voice drowns out the music: "Is he behaving? That's all you need to tell me."

I lean toward the phone and say, in a voice meant to imitate Larry's, "He's one of the finest human beans I've ever met in my life."

But Mama's too smart. "Hey, bud. Oh, golly, I can't tell you how empty I felt when I came home from work and found you gone. Mama sure misses her sweet boy. Are you being good, baby? Have they been feeding you enough?"

"Yes, ma'am."

The phone goes quiet. And in the silence I can hear her sniffling. "'Ma'am,'" she says. "Gosh, June, it certainly is nice to hear that word again. Been a long time, bud. Thank you for that."

I take the phone from Larry and punch the screen to get it out of speaker mode. "Any news, Mama?"

When she doesn't answer, I say, in maybe too desperate a tone: "Has he called or anything?"

"No, bud. No, he hasn't."

"Great. That's great. Here, talk to Larry."

I try not to listen to what he's telling her, but I have to admit it's pretty nice: how hard the boy works, how pleasant he is to be around, how kind he was to one particular client, how the younger generation might not be so bad after all.

"No, cheese has not been an issue," he says. "As a matter of fact, we just had some earlier for dessert. Cheese and grapes, red ones." He smiles at me and says, "Tell your mother bye, June."

"You tell her for me," I say, not even sure myself why I had to talk to her like that.

After saying goodbye Larry puts the phone back in his pocket. When he doesn't look at me for half an hour I know I screwed up big-time. He stands and turns up the volume on the radio, and it feels like he's doing it more for the wildflowers than for us. A few minutes later he reconsiders and turns off the radio.

"I think that could've gone better," he says, facing me at last.

"Which part?"

"The way you talked to your mother, there toward the end. That was unfortunate, June. Yes, you called her ma'am, but you could've been more respectful. You were short when you should've been gentle and patient. Ever consider what she's been through?"

"Yes, sir. All the time. She makes me consider it."

He's not done. "Through no fault of her own, she's been tasked with raising you pretty much by herself. Imagine what she experienced while your father was away fighting. The fear for him, the worry for you. Imagine her life since he's been back and now that he's vanished again. You know what I wonder? I wonder how many heads she has to cut to pay for those fancy sneakers you're wearing."

"They're not fancy. We got them at Shoe Carnival."

It's fine that he's sticking up for Mama, but it bothers me that he doesn't see that she's not the only one who's had it bad. I could throw a fit and break the Coleman lantern, or take his carburetor and toss it out in the flowers, but doing either one would only add to a picture he has of me that really isn't fair. I was just hoping Daddy had called, and it upset me when he hadn't. It wasn't Mama I was mad at.

I think he wants me to say, "Can we try again? Can we call her back?" But I'm not ready to give him that. Maybe I should grab my bag and head out for the interstate. I think I know where it is.

But he comes over now, carrying his *Artist* chair, and puts it right next to me. "Okay, June," he says, "now I'll tell you why Ford. The real reason why Ford."

"Wasn't it some genetic thing?"

"Well, sort of. Your dad's great-grandfather worked for Ford Motor Company up in Detroit and then later in Dearborn, both cities in Michigan. When he wasn't doing jobs around the plant, he worked as Henry Ford's backup chauffeur. That means he took over driving duties when the number one man, Robert Rankin, got sick or couldn't perform for whatever reason. Henry Ford had to go somewhere and Rankin couldn't rally, it was L. C. Ball who stepped up and drove him—your great-great-grandfather, June."

"All right."

"Henry Ford was not a perfect human being, but in my humble opinion his company made perfect cars. Before him automobiles were only for the rich hobbyists who could afford them. There were few on the roads—dirt roads, cobblestone roads—and they were regarded more as a nuisance than anything. Ford changed that. He created the assembly line and mass-produced them, which made them affordable for everyone. Ever hear of the Model T? Ford Motor introduced it in 1908. Ten years later half of all cars in the United States were Model Ts."

"Henry," I say. "My name is Henry, my real name."

"Yes, like your father before you, June. Both of you are Henrys. Why do you think that is?"

"My guess would have to be the old Ford guy."

"*Ding ding ding ding ding*," he says, sounding like I just got a question right on a game show. "As he got to know Henry Ford your great-great-grandpappy began to take issue with some of his views. He didn't like the false and ugly things Ford promoted about Jewish people, for instance, but he remained loyal because the job fed his family and because he came to understand that Ford the man wasn't Ford the cars. Ford the man might've been the innovator behind Ford Motor, but it was his workers who carried that company forward, along with the American people."

"L. C. Ball, huh?"

"Correct. Lawrence Cornell Ball was his full name. L. C. used to say Ford was just another name for America. Neither was without sin, but in the big picture we forgive them because we have no choice if we hope to be happy and to make others happy. A person who can't forgive or ask for forgiveness . . . in the end, June, that person only hurts himself." He reaches over and rests his hand on my arm. "I apologize for earlier, son. I was too strident, and that was wrong. You might've discovered by now that I'm the moody one, while Cornell is more easygoing."

Cornell smiles at me, his teeth shining in the moonlight.

"Also," Larry says, "I hope you'll remember that it's been a very long time since I was eleven."

"I forgive you," I say, "but only if you forgive me first."

Once we turn in for the night it is hard to sleep. The thrill of sleeping in a tent for the first time has my heart pounding, and I keep worrying that there are more than pretty wildflowers out in the field. If I saw a worm and a water bug, you know there are other things, some that I wouldn't be fast enough to run away from, others that I wouldn't know were eating me until I'd already lost a limb.

I'm thankful when Larry's phone buzzes. I see him looking at the caller's name on the screen. He lets out a long breath, as if not sure whether to answer. Cornell's been asleep for a while, at least an hour, and Larry might think I'm also asleep because I haven't moved or opened my eyes since I stretched out on my pallet and got under my sheet. He answers finally, and when he says hello, it is in a whisper.

"Are you still coming?" It is a lady, an older one. I can hear her voice even though he has the phone up to his ear.

"Yes, madam. We're working our way to you."

"There isn't much time left. I hope it's soon."

"Memphis tomorrow and then a Mustang GT in Piggott, Arkansas. A few others after that. Please trust me, Mrs. McBean. You're on our list."

"Way, way down on it."

"No, ma'am. More like the lower middle. It wouldn't be fair to all the others if we let you cut the line, would it? Besides, if your car's as bad off as you say, what's it matter if we can't get there for a few more weeks?"

"A lot," she says. "It's not how old the T-Bird is you should be worried about. It's how old Mrs. McBean is. Good night, Mr. Larry."

"Night, madam."

Larry puts down the phone and turns over on his side, away from me, and by and by I start hearing sounds that I'll do you the favor of not describing. Earlier he'd said Cornell has issues with digestion, when it turns out Cornell hasn't made a peep since we turned in.

"I'm hit," I say into my sponge pillow. I could go outside, but the bad air would just follow me, as it likes to do.

"Hit," I say again, and do my best to breathe through my mouth.

TWELVE

DADDY MIGHT'VE HAD a good sense of humor when he was young, but from what Mama told me he never did talk much. "The strong, silent type," she said. "And he wasn't ticklish. I always found that interesting. You could do under his feet, do under his arms. Do anywhere and you couldn't break him."

They met when they were students at UW Oshkosh. She walked into her English class and sat across from him and that was all it took. She had something to do at the student union after the class finished, and he followed her, panting like a little puppy, and bought her a Coke from a vending machine. She gave him her number in the dorm and told him to call if he ever needed help with a paper. They were married a year later.

Daddy dropped out not long after 9/11. "He couldn't stand to sit idly by when his country needed him," Mama said. "Then I dropped out because I had a calling, and that was hair."

The regular army wasn't enough for Daddy. He went through months of brutal training in order to become a Ranger. Daddy could parachute out of a plane four miles up in the sky and fly another sixteen miles to his desired landing zone. Once on the ground, he could navigate any kind of terrain, from mountains deep in snow to deserts with conditions so hostile scorpions hated it. You could put him in a cave in the middle of the forest with a compass and nothing else and he could find his way home. In hand-to-hand combat he could stop the enemy without things ever having to get messy. Mama got so anxious every time he left on another mission she could barely cut a straight line. She messed up a lot, snipping off places her clients didn't want snipped. By the time I came along, Daddy was already drinking too much, even while on base. We'd go to the commissary some days and he'd fill the cart with beer, nothing but beer.

I was five when he got his first DUI, six when he got his second. The army gave him an honorable discharge along with his chestful of medals, and we pulled a rented trailer behind his pickup and moved back to our pretty little town on the Sheboygan River. I don't remember many fights when we were in Georgia, but I did see them on Hickory Street— broken cabinet doors, holes in the Sheetrock.

The neighbors loved us, regardless. Whenever Mama cooked a big meal she brought leftovers to Mr. Kunz. Sometimes I went with her. He's a widower and too old and crippled to do his own cooking or to go out for food. I could tell from his expression that he felt sorry for us, when we should've been feeling sorry for him.

"Thank you for not calling anybody," I heard Mama tell him once as she handed over another half pan of meat loaf. I knew she meant the police.

"I don't know what I'd do without you," Daddy used to tell her, when he was getting over a bad spell.

"Wuv you, too," she'd say, I guess because that was easier than "I love you," especially after a fight.

We're back on the interstate heading south. Through the windshield I can see the road fattening as we drive to meet it. Broken streaks of white paint decorate the middle, and the black shoulders bubble in the heat.

The trees look bigger and spookier than the ones we have back home. Cornell says these are Southern live oaks and "they're some big old boys and girls, all right." I like the blues music on the radio, the harmonicas moaning, guitars crying like the end of the world has come. There are billboards everywhere, a lot of them for restaurants selling barbecue.

We pull into Memphis, Tennessee, and stop in front of a store in an older part of town. A metal sign attached to the building says DICKIES. I'm thinking I'll wait in the truck, but Larry and Cornell tell me to come with them.

There's a guy sleeping on a sheet of cardboard not far away.

I don't mean to put him down by wondering if he's a home-less person, but he's the first one I've ever seen. If only I had a dollar, I would give it to him.

The uniform store is stuck in a time warp, where there's no such thing as Amazon or even shopping malls. You wonder how they stay open. We file in, and an old man and an old lady come out from behind a glass counter to greet us. The lady takes Larry's face in her hands and pats it on both sides, while the man gives Cornell the same treatment.

"And this is cousin June?" the lady says. "My, what a cute guy."

So she knows me, this person with hair in a frosty beehive and an ink-stained tape measure hanging around her neck.

How is that?

The lady keeps looking me up and down, and she taps the points of my shoulders as if to make them not quite so wide. While she's doing this, the man goes to a shelf and grabs a package wrapped in brown paper.

"For you, June," Larry says.

"For me?"

"That's correct. Open it."

I tear the paper off, and it's two pairs of coveralls just like theirs. Both of them have *Ball Garage* in big letters sewn across the back and blue oval patches on the sleeves. My name in red thread is on the patch over the pocket. *June Ball*, it says, rather than Henry Ball Jr., which I would've preferred, although I'm not complaining.

"What do you think?" the lady says. "You like?"

I never really knew what being overwhelmed felt like until now. "Yes," I whisper. "I like."

"Thought we should get you two of them," Cornell says, "so you'll have a spare when one gets so dirty you can't stand wearing it anymore."

They point to the dressing room, and I stumble back to it with the coveralls, making sure the leg bottoms don't drag on the linoleum. The room is small but lined with mirrors, which makes it seem like an army of identical June Balls just stepped inside. Both pairs of coveralls are the same size, so I need to try only one on. The material's as stiff as cardboard, but it's a good fit except for the shoulders, which might be a little tight. I look at myself in the glass and can hardly believe it. I look so different I squint to make sure it's really me.

I put my shoes on and leave the dressing room, and they all start clapping and carrying on. You wonder how models put up with it.

I feel like the Ball Garage mascot, but that's okay.

"Need more room?" the lady says and taps my shoulders again. "Not too tight?"

"I think I'm good."

"Yeah, he's good," Larry says. "The Ball men and their big shoulders. Just something he'll have to get used to."

"Now for some of these," Cornell says, holding up one of his boots. "You don't want to ruin your sneakers, do you?"

The man from the store measures my feet, then goes in the

back. I've walked around the house in Daddy's boots before, once or twice, when he wasn't looking, but I never thought I'd own my own. The man comes out with a box that's twice as big as the usual kind for sneakers. He sits on a low stool in front of me and removes the boot for the right foot. He helps me get it on, then he helps me get the left one on.

"Walk around, see how they feel," he says.

You wouldn't believe how tall they make me, with those heels. The man puts my sneakers in the boot box, then he puts the box in a paper bag that already holds my spare coveralls and the clothes I was wearing when we came in.

"A new you," he says. "You like? I hope you like."

Once we're outside, Larry says it's where he and Cornell have been buying their coveralls for years. They always stop when they're in the area. Larry placed the order from his phone before we left Sheboygan Falls, and he and Cornell charged it to their account.

"I can't believe you did that for me," I say, and I can tell they like hearing it. "Cousin Larry? Cousin Cornell? Thank you. Thank you so much."

We're walking to the truck, and the guy on the cardboard is still there. He whistles as we move past him.

"'Preciate that," I tell him, because I know the whistle is meant for me.

Cornell gets a new batch of deviled eggs from the truck—the ones he made before we broke down the campsite this morning. He stands over the guy, holding the tray, and the guy takes one, sniffs it a few times, then puts it in his mouth. He's a slow eater. It's like he doesn't want to swallow, knowing that it would be the end to his momentary pleasure.

"Delicious," he says, looking up after he gets it down.

"Go on, have some more," Cornell says. And he gives him the whole tray.

Next we drive by the place where Elvis Presley lived. He was a singer unlike any around today, Cornell explains. There was a popular TV show on Sunday nights and he went on it a few times, and they had to film him from the waist up because in those days to shake your hips in public the way he did got you in hot water with the federal government. You could go to jail. Years after he died, people still like him so much they come from all over to see his house, which is called Graceland.

I never do see the place, although we drive by it. It's behind a stone wall and set way back from the road, and several Greyhounds are parked in front, blocking the view. Plus, when you're moving at a fast clip you have to know what to look for, and I didn't. I saw the buses, the wall, a bunch of grass and trees, and a long section of white fence.

"Incredible, huh?" Cornell says.

When I don't answer, Larry says, "You didn't see it?"

"Where?"

"You want me to turn around?" It's Cornell again. "Because I will; I'll turn around."

"No, I saw it," I say, because that's what he needs to hear.

"You can't visit Memphis without visiting Graceland," Larry says.

"Grateful to you for showing it to me. I'm sure I'll never forget it."

There was also a guard shack. I should mention that. I definitely saw the shack, and I think I might've seen a guard.

Next we go to the Peabody and stop and get out this time. It's an old hotel full of history that we're in too big a hurry to learn about, mainly because we used up all of our spare time driving past Graceland.

The Peabody's lobby makes you feel like you're in a palace in another country. It is that nice. You walk around with your mouth open until you come to a mob standing around a large marble fountain where some ducks are swimming. I'm wondering who let them in, and then I see a man in a red jacket with gold buttons using a cane to try to get the ducks out of the water. The ducks don't want to cooperate, and so the man is making them. He unfurls a long rug that's the same color as his outfit. It runs from the fountain all the way across the lobby to the elevators. The rug is for the ducks.

I finally put it together that the ducks are trained performers. They're like rock stars, like Elvis must've been. That's why the kids start screaming when the birds leave the water and why everybody takes their picture with cameras and cell phones. A voice comes over an intercom and explains that the ducks have been performing at the hotel every day since the 1930s. *Those are some old ducks*, I think. They live in the

Royal Duck Palace on the rooftop, which is why they need the elevator. Today there are only four of them, three brown females and one big, colorful male. One of the lady ducks seems to be in charge.

As we stand over by the elevator watching, some of the crowd seems more interested in us than in the ducks. It has to be the coveralls.

"Thank you, thank you very much," Larry and Cornell say when one gal takes our picture.

I don't realize that they're talking like Elvis until somebody mentions it. He actually says, "Oh, I get it. Two bald-headed Elvises and a little pint-size Elvis." Which would be me.

"Thank you, thank you very much," Larry and Cornell say again.

The ducks and the duck master walk right past us into a waiting elevator. And then as soon as the doors close and they head upstairs, the mob makes a circle around us, everybody taking selfies with us now.

"Thank you, thank you very much," I say. And the people laugh like it's the funniest thing they ever heard.

It takes half an hour to get into an elevator, and our faces are smudged with lipstick, and my hand hurts from all the shaking we had to do.

We go up to the rooftop for an appointment with an assistant manager, Mr. Rice, who's preparing for a party later tonight.

He tells us he owns a 1947 Ford woody wagon, which he

bought just recently from a guest of the hotel. The guest drove up to valet parking, and Mr. Rice noticed the FOR SALE sign taped to the windshield, and he automatically remembered back to his dad's old woody. His dad was deceased, he was sad to report, and the woody was long gone, and Mr. Rice felt such a surge of emotion that he wrote a check for the woody on the spot. Now he regrets being so impulsive. "I grew up in Southern California," he says. "My first thought was, wouldn't it look great with a surfboard on top? Dumb me, where can you go surfing in Memphis? The closest beach is five hundred miles away. But we do get rain in Memphis, tons of it. And the wood on the car, which is either maple or mahogany, has begun to rot." He forms a prayer steeple with his hands. "I was hoping you could help me with that."

"Mr. Rice, we'd love to help you, but we're mechanics, not body guys," Cornell says.

"There's nothing seriously wrong with the mechanicals," Mr. Rice says, "but I found termites—*termites*, can you believe?"

"I could've recommended a body shop when we spoke on the phone," Larry says, "but you didn't mention termites. And I never heard of bugs eating up a woody—they don't usually like the various woods Ford used in their cars. Now I'm starting to think what you really need is an exterminator."

"Yeah. And a furniture repairman," Cornell says.

My cousins don't sound like they mean to poke fun, but Mr. Rice takes it that way. "Just what are you saying, Balls?"

"Nothing," Larry answers, "except that you should've called Orkin."

They keep discussing it, the three of them, and I walk over and look at the house where the ducks live. They've got a nice setup if you're a person but probably not if you're a duck. There's an iron fence where you can look out past the city's rooftops to the Mississippi River. I stand next to it and get a little light-headed just looking. The river is quite a thing to see from this high up, with the sun hitting the surface and making it sparkle. I wonder if the ducks have their wings clipped. I bet if they saw the river they would try to fly to it and get away. I know that's what I'd do if I were a duck.

Larry and Cornell come for me after a while, and we take the elevator back down with Mr. Rice and walk over to a parking area.

The woody has its own reserved spot, and I can see what Mr. Rice meant about the termites. There are trails running through the wood on the sides. He pushes his thumb against a panel, and it crackles and splits, and sawdust falls to the pavement.

"Why continue to make cars out of wood when we can make them out of American steel?" Larry says. "Beginning in the fifties, Ford started asking that question. To keep the wood look, which people liked, Ford's answer was to paste on decals. These decals simulated wood grain, but even from a distance you could tell they were fake. Mr. Rice, don't get upset with me when I repeat what Cornell said earlier, but you have a very strange situation here, and I think a furniture restorer is your answer. I knew termites were a big problem down south, but who ever heard of them eating a car?"

Mr. Rice shakes his head. It looks like his mouth is full and he might need to spit. I don't think he's remembering back to good times with his dad anymore.

"It's eating me alive that we can't help," Larry says.

"Another joke, Ball?"

"No, sir. Forgive me. That didn't come out right."

I don't think Mr. Rice believes him. He really does spit now, then he walks to the lobby and goes inside, big glass doors whooshing closed behind him.

"There's at least one every summer," Larry says. "Best not to dwell on it."

"I was thinking Mr. Rice could go to the lumberyard and get some boards and nail them along the sides," I say. "Would that work?"

They both look at me at the same time, and tears shine in their eyes. I figure the tears are for the woody, not the cranky guy who owns it.

"Hey, how do those Dickies feel?" Larry asks, trying to cheer things up.

"Good," I answer. "Really good."

"Shoulders loosening up?"

"Yes, sir."

"Boots aren't giving you blisters, are they?"

"No, sir," I answer, and hold one up. "But even if they did I still wouldn't take them off."

THIRTEEN

I THINK I FIGURED OUT how to stop looking for my dad. Instead I look for those trees Mama talked about, the ones with holes in their trunks, but it turns out they're not around, either. Most trees, if you were to carve out holes in them, wouldn't be wide enough to ride a bike through. Some you couldn't get through walking sideways.

We are driving to a place in northeastern Arkansas called Piggott, about two hours away. Larry says there's a classic Mustang we need to fix.

We stop for gas, and I go inside to use the restroom. When I return to the truck the stupid bucket with the stupid carburetor is on the seat.

"Really?" I say, giving them both nasty looks.

"Got a little driving time ahead of us," Larry says. "Thought you might like to practice."

He's holding two screwdrivers—"This one's your flathead, and this one here is your Phillips"—and he makes me feel the ends with my fingers. I understand that he's trying to teach me, but I'm just not in a carburetor mood. The word *flathead* makes me think of a flat iron, one of the important tools Mama uses at the salon. If I'd only thought to pack one I could be lecturing Larry now on how to straighten hair.

"Can I play with your phone instead?" I say.

"Not just yet."

"The Holley's too hard. I think my fingers are too fat."

"I thought you liked it." He's sounding wounded, and he's looking it, too. His lower lip is pooching out.

"With Daddy it was football," I say. "He played in high school, and you couldn't get through a Packers game without him sitting in front of the TV and pointing out pass routes and coverages. Out route. Dig route. Man. Zone. Used to bore me to tears with all that."

"But you grew to like it, didn't you?"

"Only because he did."

"See there." He gives the bucket a shake. "Come on. Don't give up yet."

I get started, and it's not as bad as before. As each screw comes out, I hand it to him and he puts it in a food storage container and snaps the lid shut. Outside there's not much to look at unless you like fields and little brick houses and dogs in wire pens. By the time a road sign says Piggott is fifty miles away, I've taken the carburetor completely apart. Some of the bigger pieces rest on the seat between us. Others are scattered on the floor.

"Very good," Larry says. "Now let's see if you can put it back together before we reach Mrs. Barnwell's."

Mrs. Barnwell owns a big modern house made mostly of glass, and she herself also seems very modern. I think Mama would like her inverted bob. The only problem I see with it is a small stain on her scalp where the dye ran. I must've picked up more than I thought hanging out at the Déjà Do. Thinking about Mama now makes me wish I could sweep up the hair on the floor at her booth. The sight of a lady with interesting hair must have me missing home.

The Mustang convertible is parked on the side of the house, and Mrs. Barnwell starts walking around it, her nose way up in the air to make sure you understand how special she is.

"I was a runner-up in the Miss America pageant and came home from Atlantic City to find it parked in the driveway with a red ribbon around it and a big bow on the roof," she says. "My parents couldn't afford it, but they were over-the-moon proud, and they thought they'd celebrate my triumph by surprising me with the sweetest car on the road. The town threw me a parade, and I rode sitting on top of the back seat, waving at everybody. I haven't driven it in years. With the fiftieth anniversary of my reign as Miss Arkansas coming up, the town wants to recognize me. The mayor thought my presence in the parade might be meaningful to young girls in search of a role model. His office got excited when they heard I still owned the Mustang. I've been watching my calories and doing aerobics with a girl from California on the computer, but I haven't done anything with the car yet. My ex-husband wasn't any good with his hands. My dream is to have him and his new wife see me getting the cheers. There's all this applause from fans old and new, and I look so good he gets confused and forgets what year it is."

Larry and Cornell patiently listen. They nod the whole time she's talking, and neither interrupts once, but I do notice their eyes are on the car.

She still hasn't finished her Academy Award–acceptance speech when Larry and Cornell get started. They open the doors and have a look at the interior, then they pop the hood and lean over the engine, touching it in different places.

"Will you start it for us, Mrs. Barnwell?" Larry says.

Her voice trails off just as she was giving the number of times her picture ran in the paper. She gets behind the wheel and inserts the key, and it takes a few tries before the engine catches. Larry and Cornell resume their positions under the hood and start touching things again.

"Okay, turn it off now," Larry says.

"You didn't say 'please,'" Mrs. Barnwell says.

"Please," Cornell says, and smiles at her.

Once it's finally quiet Larry and Cornell wipe their hands on their shop rags.

"Mrs. Barnwell, your hoses leak," Cornell says.

"They do?"

"Yes, ma'am. Leak bad. You'll want to replace them."

"June, my hoses leak," she tells me, pretending she can't believe it.

"Your valve cover gaskets," Cornell says next. "They need to go, too."

"Anything else while you're breaking my heart?"

"Your radiator. I'm sorry, Mrs. Barnwell."

"No! Not him!" She steps over to where they're standing and pokes her head under the hood. "Okay, show me where's the radiator."

Larry points to it, then holds his right hand up with three fingers poking out. "Three days. But that could change depending on what other issues we find and how fast we can get parts. We'll need to have them overnighted, if that's all right with you."

"Yes, it's fine."

"You'll pay the FedEx fees? Ain't cheap."

"Yes. Anything you need as long as it's ready in time for the parade."

"Just so you know," Cornell says, "we'll be installing klieg lights on tall stands and placing them around the car. They'll come on at dark and stay on until morning. It's an early evening when we shut down before midnight. Some days it's dawn. The generator will be running at all hours, and it's loud, Mrs. Barnwell, bad loud."

The whole time Cornell is talking, Mrs. Barnwell stares

at him in a way that's hard to describe. It's almost as if Cornell is making Mrs. Barnwell hungry.

"By the way," she says, "you're more than welcome to stay in the mother-in-law suite. There are two full beds and a couch that pulls out."

"Grateful for the offer, but it's against our policy," Larry says. "We'll just stay in the yard."

"Really? In the yard? In *my* yard?"

"We have a tent. I was wondering if there's a spot where you'd prefer we put our privy?"

She turns away from Cornell and stares at Larry. "Your who-vy?"

"Our privy, madam. Because of our odd hours, we'd rather not be a nuisance and tramp in and out of your house. No worries, Mrs. Barnwell. We'll fill in the hole when we're done and replace the sod. You'll never know we were there."

"I have four bathrooms in the house. The one in the suite makes five. You'd be able to come and go as you please. Won't bother me in the least."

"Thank you," Larry says, "but I'm afraid we must insist. Policy, madam."

"In that case, over there." She points to an area where the grass is already dead. "Looks like it could use the fertilizer."

I help them haul the tent out of the back, then I help them put it up. When we finish, Cornell says, "Time to test those shoulders."

The spot for the privy is by the rear fence where there are no tree roots to chop through. Cornell gets the hole started, and I watch how he handles the shovel. He uses his weight to drive the blade into the ground, then when he lifts the dirt out he does so with his upper body, legs, and rear end, using all three at once. For a guy with a pencil neck and hardly any muscles, he's incredibly strong. He tries to soften his grunts, but it only makes him sound like somebody getting beat up. I like how the soil smells combined with the smell of the cedar fence. I wonder if it's the last time things won't reek back here.

When it's my turn I dig another few feet down, making the same noises Cornell did.

"Okay, June, deep enough," Larry says. He takes some of the dirt and rubs it in his hands. "Ford is just a name for what?" he says.

"America," I answer. It's hard to talk because I'm worn out from the digging.

Larry wraps a hand around his ear. "I didn't hear you. Louder, June. Another name for *what*?"

"*America!*" And I really shout this time, so loud Mrs. Barnwell steps out in the yard to see if somebody chopped off a toe.

Next we put up the four fiberglass panels that make up the privy walls. Basically, it's a tall box around the hole. The door is the one facing the house with the hook-and-eye latch and the isinglass porthole.

To finish the job, Cornell gets the toilet seat and strides out with it, moving right past Mrs. Barnwell. Not that I'd ever mention this to him and Larry, but the seat's the same oval shape as the Ford oval. Cornell fits it on a frame made of light-weight aluminum pipe that forms the legs. "You know what they call a privy down under?" Larry asks me.

"No, sir."

"Thunderbox. They actually call it that. I kid you not."

"Did the GPS navigator tell you that?"

"No. All he ever tells us is where to go, but it's never to that place."

Ours has an exhaust pipe that runs from the hole in the ground all the way up to a tar paper roof, and a second pipe, fitted into a side wall about halfway up, allows air from outside to flow in. These pipes form a ventilation system to make sure nobody dies from the fumes.

The last thing Cornell carries out is a bag of lime. The way it works is that when you finish you sprinkle some down into the hole.

I probably shouldn't be including all these details, but I'm sure you've wondered. And it's okay, because everybody wonders.

The shower, which we install next, is a similar construction of seven-foot-tall panels forming a box. We run a garden hose from a spigot at the side of the house and attach it to the top with a spring clamp, the nozzle pointing down. You turn on the water and then run and get in. You use soap and shampoo like anywhere else.

Not so bad.

It's almost dark when Larry and Cornell start work on the Mustang. I must be yawning too much because they tell me to take a break.

"You're growing," Cornell says. "That takes a lot out of a young person."

I don't want them to think of me as a lightweight, but the work really is exhausting, even when you're just standing around.

How do they not get tired? How do they go so long without sleep?

I don't remember asking them these questions, but Larry turns to me and says, "Oh, we sleep. We sleep plenty. Don't you worry about that. But getting the Mustang ready in time for the parade has our adrenaline flowing. You know what adrenaline is, son?"

"Heard of it."

"It's a hormone produced by the adrenal glands, which are here." He points to the middle of his back. "Not sure exactly how to explain what a hormone is, but I know this particular one helps gets your heart pumping, and you get a rush of energy. That rush is . . ."

"Adrenaline?" I say. I think I pronounce it right.

Mrs. Barnwell is sitting on her patio. She must have adrenaline in her eyeballs. It's been hours since she took them off Cornell.

"You don't find her kind of weird?" I say. "That story about getting back at her husband?"

"Not weird, no. But sad, yes. Very, very sad. Seems to me she put her hand in the wrong toolbox and pulled out the wrong ruler to measure her value. We're going to get her car to run again—oh, you can count on that—but it's going to take more than a parade for Mrs. Barnwell to understand what really makes her special."

He goes back to help Cornell, and I crawl in the tent and dig in my bag for *The Red Pony*. I start reading by the glow of the klieg lights.

I've never ridden a horse, but it's something I'd like to do one day. Even touching one would be good. I bet it's hot being a horse, all that hair. All that running and somebody on your back smacking you with a whip or kicking you with spurs. It turns out the pony in the book has red fur and a gray nose. Horses must be like people, where you basically have the color spectrum, which is pretty neat if you ask me. You know how this works: One minute you're turning a page, the next it's morning and the sun is already in the trees.

I sit up and look through the open tent flaps. Mrs. Barnwell has moved her patio chair to the middle of the yard. She's still wearing what she had on yesterday. So are Larry and Cornell, for that matter, but their outfits never change except in the amount of dirt and grease that stains them.

I'm sure it's not the first time my cousins attracted an admiring audience. There are several wine bottles at Mrs. Barnwell's feet—well, two of them, both tumbled over in the grass. I swear I'll never drink when I get old. Why do it if it makes you weird?

"Oh, Daddy," I whisper, suddenly remembering.

Mrs. Barnwell starts laughing. Do not ask me why. Nothing happened just then that hadn't been happening a while ago, unless it happened in her head.

"Went from one venue to the next in limos," she says, in a sort of shout. "First class all the way. Best sheets on your bed, best soaps, best food even though all of us were laying off carbs until it was over. My escort was a young Wall Street trader, had his shirts made by an Italian tailor who always put his monogram right here on the cuff. What was that boy's name? Oh heck! Why can't I remember anymore?"

She throws her head back, and her bob looks like a football helmet about to fly off. I keep wishing I had an iPod and some earbuds to spare me all this.

"Oh, Cornie," Mrs. Barnwell says, though more to the sky than Cornell.

He and Larry stop working. They stand next to the Mustang watching her. Cornell whispers in Larry's ear, then Larry drops his pliers and comes walking toward me. At the door to the tent he squats and looks in. "Glad you were able to enjoy some quiet time, June. Would you help me with a situation, please?" He's being very calm. "I'd like to escort Mrs. Barnwell back to the house and get her inside. Better you and me than cousin Cornell."

"She's in love with him," I blurt out.

He doesn't answer, unless you count the misery in his eyes.

We stand on either side of her and hook her under her arms.

"Ready, madam?" Larry says.

Then we lift her out of the chair. She offers no resistance, and she isn't heavy, nothing like Daddy when Mama and I would have to haul him in from the porch.

"Am I too old?" she says. "Is that it? Do I really *smell* old? He told one of his friends that." She holds her arm out for Larry and me to smell. I'm not sure I smell anything. Some lotion, maybe.

We reach the house, and Larry gets the door open. We turn sideways and get the job done that way.

It's a living room with a ceiling as tall as an airport terminal. She definitely likes white: white couches, white chairs, white tables, white rug. Even the paintings on the walls are white, with matching white frames. We get her to sit down, and it's a relief because I was about to drop her.

"Police escorts everywhere we went. Sirens and swirling lights. He sent me a telegram saying he loved me. The boy from Wall Street had invited me to dinner, but I told him sorry, I couldn't, I already had someone." For some reason she points at me. "Be careful what you wish for, June. You just might get it. And then what?"

I can't tell if she's expecting an answer, but in the end I don't have to give her one. She kicks off her shoes, falls back, and goes to sleep. Larry gets a blanket from one of the chairs and covers her with it.

Do I even have to tell you what color it is?

Because of the situation, Larry and Cornell decide to make it a two-day rather than a three-day job—once the FedEx truck arrives and drops off the parts they ordered.

They show me where the hoses are leaking, why the radiator needs to be replaced, and how to put on valve cover gaskets. Then they have me watch them change the oil, which is my favorite of all the chores.

First you get on the ground under the engine and slide toward the middle, where there's a drain plug. You put your pan under this plug—you always want to remember to bring your pan. You unscrew the plug, and all the dirty oil flows out and into the pan. Take the pan away and then screw the plug back in. Then add your oil. You can tell when it's at the right level by checking your stick, which is basically a skinny ruler a couple of feet long that shows you where your oil level needs to be. As you're doing all this, you need to remember to change your filter. You don't get to the filter from where you were down on the ground under the engine. Instead you get at it from the top.

"It's right there," Cornell says. "See it?"

"Yes, sir."

"That's your filter. It will still have oil in it, so you want to be careful as you're removing it. Here, watch me. See my rag in case it wants to spill? See I brought my bucket? You lower your old filter right in here. See how I'm doing that? Then you put your new filter on."

Our next chores are to make sure the convertible top works and to clean the interior with shop rags and protectant. They also get me to wash her the way I did the Ranchero. They're relaxing in the shade of a mimosa tree now, the only break I've seen them take since we got here.

"Good remembering," they say, when I remember to work from the top down.

Mrs. Barnwell never does apologize for that first night, but she does try to make up for it by bringing us food. There are burgers and baked chicken breasts, sausage pizzas, and assorted fruit pies, all of them homemade. We eat on the ground under the tree, legs folded beneath us, Chinet plates centered on our laps.

"Here, son, try the apple," Larry says. And he gives me a piece even though I just had slices of lemon and blueberry.

The more I think about Mrs. Barnwell, the more I feel sorry for her. She can never be that beauty contestant again, no matter how stylish her hair is or how much dye she puts in it. Cornell gets quiet every time she shuffles out with something new to eat. He doesn't speak to her until we're almost ready to leave, when she brings out fizzy water in green bottles.

"Fancy water," she calls it, "because we need to celebrate and I know better than to offer champagne."

Cornell takes a sip, and the bubbles make him make a funny face. "It sure must take a lot of courage to ride in a convertible in a sparkly dress and gloves up to your elbows, waving at strangers," he says.

She smiles at him. "Courage? Well, I never thought of it that way, but, yes, I suppose I can see your point."

"Me myself, I could never do it. I'm sorry we're going to miss the parade. That would've been a memorable experience for all concerned. I know you'll do great."

Cornell tries the water again and makes the same face, and Larry says, "Forgive us, Mrs. Barnwell, but another Ford beckons."

"They beckon?"

"Yes, ma'am." He has a napkin hanging from the neck of his coveralls. He wipes his mouth with it. "When you're out making new friends, you wouldn't believe how fast the time passes. It goes and so do you, always right behind it but never quite able to catch up."

Mrs. Barnwell takes a minute to think about that. "Larry," she says, "what if you drive the Mustang and we come from up the street over there?" She points. "Cornie and June can watch from the yard. It's been so long, I could use the practice."

Larry and Cornell both glance at their watches. "Only if we do it now, madam," Larry says.

He and Mrs. Barnwell get in the car and ride up the street together. He uses somebody's driveway to turn around, then he points the Mustang in our direction. Cornell and I walk over to the middle of the yard and stand next to each other. I usually get excited at a parade, but not so much today.

They're a good distance up the street, the length of two football fields at least, but I can see her move to where she's sitting up on the back seat. She starts waving even before Larry starts driving. It's only one hand, and it's one of those robotic scoop waves that beauty queens do. I never understood why any girl would want to be a princess, let alone a queen, but that is just one of those mysteries I have the rest of my life to solve.

The street has nobody on it—no cars, no people—so Larry drives the Mustang straight down the middle. Mrs. Barnwell is sitting up higher than the top of the windshield, and there's enough wind to throw her hair back and flatten her clothes against her body. I'd put their speed at less than a mile an hour.

As she comes closer she pretends to just now spot us in a crowd. Both hands go up and the scoops intensify. Her invisible evening gown shimmers in the sun, and the invisible diamonds in her invisible crown shoot off invisible sparks.

I'm good at whistling, so I uncork one. Cornell doesn't seem to know what to do, but at the last second, as they're moving past us, he brings the flat of his hand up to his mouth, touches his lips with it, and blows Mrs. Barnwell a kiss.

She catches it and holds it against her heart.

You'd think his kind gesture would make her feel good, but the Mustang has come to a stop, and all we see her do is sob.

"Her apple pie might be the best I ever had," Larry says on our way out of town. But Cornell doesn't hear him.

He's sleeping with his head against the door.

FOURTEEN

WE MAKE STOPS IN ENID, Ardmore, and Okemah, all good Ford towns in Oklahoma. Then in Mississippi it's Eupora and Clarksdale.

We work on a Del Rio, a Model 48, a Skyliner, a Vanette, and a Pinto. We camp behind a church and a skating rink, and in a cemetery, a salvage yard, and the courtyard of a small animal hospital where they must let the patients use the bathroom. We unload the tent and the thunderbox and then load them back up again. Late at night and early in the morning, we sing along to songs on the radio as we zigzag from one stop to the next on gravel, shell, dirt, asphalt, and concrete, the Aussie on the GPS telling us where to go.

"We have the phone and the map, so it's unlikely we'll ever get lost," Larry says, "but if you ever do, pause for a moment and listen to how people talk. Accents can change from one town to the next. Further south, they'll sound like English royalty in one place, but you drive ten miles down the road and it's Cajun, which has roots in French Canada. By recalling each accent and assigning it to a particular region, you can figure out where you are."

I might not know my accents yet, but I can distinguish one noise from another in the back of the truck. The rattling, for instance, is the walls of the thunderbox and the shower rubbing together. The knock-knock-knocking is the GOD FORD sign bouncing against the bulkhead. The sound of waves crashing on the beach is melted ice sloshing around in the coolers.

We do a Mainline Ranch Wagon in Dumas, Arkansas. The owner makes his own jelly from mayhaw berries that grow on trees in his yard. Before we leave he gives us a big mason jar full of the stuff, and we stop at the Piggly Wiggly on the way out and buy a loaf of bread and gorge on jelly sandwiches in the parking lot. After we wipe out the bread, there's still some jelly left. We eat it with our fingers.

"Dumas, Arkansas," I yell out the window, "I shall never forget thee."

Larry and Cornell both start to answer but burp instead, their mouths ringed with jelly.

Our next stop is Bastrop.

"When we were leaving Wisconsin did you ever imagine making it all the way to Louisiana, June?" Cornell says.

"Louisiana? How did that happen?"

"Don't ask me. I'm just driving."

There are several big gas stations where we exit, each one lit up with computerized pumps equipped with TVs advertising malt liquor and lottery tickets. Cornell drives past them and stops at a little mom-and-pop painted bright yellow and covered in advertising signs. A few of these signs are decorated with boots—the shape of the state with the foot part pointing eastward. The station has only two pumps, both relics with dents and sun-bleached paint.

I go in the store and use the men's room. The good news is how clean it is, the floors still damp from a recent mopping. Even the soap dispenser is full. I wash my hands and inhale a familiar scent—Pine-Sol, the same stuff Mama uses back home. If I could change one thing about the trip it would be the thunderbox. The deal is, you have to look down the hole in order to aim right when you're pouring the lime. I could pass out every time I have to do that.

I leave the men's room, and the old guy at the register says, "Where y'all headed, if you don't mind me asking?"

"I don't know. They haven't told me."

The man is glaring out the window. "That's an F6 cab-over with a customized back end, ain't it?"

"Yes, sir, I think that's right."

"Cargo box is double the size of any I've ever seen before. That thing is a monster. Y'all hauling heavy machinery?"

"No, sir. We're just out fixing Fords."

"Fixing Fords, are you?"

I nod and step to the side. Another customer needs to pay for her Funyuns.

The old guy takes her money and makes change, and

after she's gone he says, "I'm an Oldsmobile man myself, but I can forgive you this once. We all got to be something, don't we, son?"

"Yes, sir, I suppose that's true."

"Listen, I couldn't get you to go back in the toilet and shake the handle, could I? You don't hear that water running?"

I go in and shake it and come back out, and Larry is at the counter counting out cash for the gas. Then he remembers that we need ice and adds more bills to the pile.

"You got yourself a fine boy there, mister," the man says.

Larry stammers a little, like he's about to correct him, but then he looks back in my direction and our eyes meet. "Yes, I do," he says. "A very fine boy. Thank you for saying so."

Olla, Urania, and Tullos come next. They really do have some interesting names in the state of Louisiana.

This is just something I've noticed—I'm not being critical—but if we have to dodge another dead possum in the road, I swear I'm going to lose it.

Besides the possums, all we keep seeing are pine trees, miles and miles of them. They're tall and skinny, with the crowns two hundred feet up, and they must count in the millions. When the wind blows, they bend forward all at once, and it's almost like they're curtsying before the queen.

Hawks sit on telephone lines that run along the road. I wonder if their entertainment is watching the possums get smacked. A lumber truck turns in front of us and strains to pull its load, red dust spiraling behind it and forcing Cornell to turn on the wipers.

"There it is," he says, and points to a sign that says PINEVILLE.

"A town named right if there ever was one," Larry says.

Cornell brings the speed down, and Larry taps out a text on his phone. We stop at a malt-and-burger place with picnic tables under a lean-to. The lot is full of dusty pickups with magnetic signs on the doors for plumbers and air-conditioning repairmen. Cornell buys a round of root beer floats, and we sit in the hot shade, eating with long-handled spoons that bend against the sticky weight of the ice cream. I'd tell you the name of the joint, in case you're ever down this way, but the only sign is a board in the shape of a burger with the menu painted on it.

A sheriff's deputy pulls up and takes the spot next to our truck. He steps out, putting a khaki-colored hat on, then he walks toward where we're sitting.

"Royal," I hear somebody say at a table close to ours, and the cop acknowledges the man with a finger wave.

The cop must figure out who we are. "Royal Dauterive," he says, gliding over in his highly polished shoes. All three of us stand and shake his hand, and before I can tell him who I am he says, "And you must be June."

Does it freak me out that a cop knows my name? Not at all. Larry must've told him about me when they were scheduling our visit.

Cornell gathers up our empty cups and drops them in a trash can. Larry and I move out of the shade and into the lot.

I'm about to ask Mr. Dauterive why there are so many pine trees when Larry says, "I sure hope we can help you. Should be able to. Always relish the opportunity to get my hands on an early Falcon."

"I can't tell you how grateful my wife and I are to you, sir. Janice and me, we're a single-income operation, so it's always a challenge. Listen, why don't y'all follow me? We're just on the other side of the highway."

He reaches up again for his hat, intending to take it off before he gets back in his cruiser, and that is when I see it under his watch: There's a *Sua Sponte* tattoo on his wrist, barely visible against his dark skin.

It's exactly like my dad's.

My finger's shaking when I lift it and point. "What's that, Mr. Dauterive? Your tattoo there?"

"Oh, that," he says, as if he'd forgotten he even had it. "Just a youthful indiscretion, I think might be the best description. Bunch of the guys and myself went and got them. Rangers really aren't supposed to have tattoos, but they're so small we could hide them under our watches. Janice keeps telling me it needs to come off. I told her I could never."

"Were you ever stationed at Fort Benning?"

He stares at me but doesn't answer right away. "Yes, I was, June."

"The Seventy-Fifth Ranger Regiment, then, right?"

He nods.

"Did you ever run into my dad, by chance? Henry Ball Sr.? He was a Ranger, too. He had that same tattoo."

"No, I don't recall ever meeting your father. Do you have any idea how many military personnel operate out of Benning at any given time? Thousands, June. We must've been in different battalions."

"I've been trying to find him."

"What do you mean, you're trying to find him? He left home, did he?"

"Yes, sir. He took off about five months ago. We haven't heard from him since, my mother and me."

He gives me another long look. "Henry Ball Sr.," he says, his voice quieter than before. "I can ask around. Maybe somebody will know him, but a lot of us served, June, and a lot of us got these tattoos. It was the thing to do for about ten minutes. Kind of silly, now that I think about it."

I make sure not to look away from him. "Anything you can do, Mr. Dauterive, I'd appreciate it."

"Just had to have it if my buddies did, you know?"

"Yes, sir. My dad used to say the same thing."

We follow his cruiser out of the lot, and I'm throbbing all over. My heart beats in my ears, and sweat trickles down my rib cage.

"If you don't look, you don't find, huh, June?" Cornell says.

It might be the perfect way to put it. I'd let him know that if only I still had the ability to speak.

★ ★ ★

Mr. Dauterive's neighborhood reminds me of mine. The houses are small and boxy, everybody keeps their yards up, and plants hanging from chains decorate the front porches and swing in the breeze. There are lots of pines here, too, but mixed in are other, smaller trees, most of them holding bunches of tiny pink and white flowers. Don't take this to the bank, but I think those smaller trees are named after a lady named Myrtle.

"Client Royal Dauterive, decorated veteran, owns a 1964 Ford Falcon Sprint. It's actually his wife's car, inherited from her late father, who himself was a Vietnam-era war hero. If they can get the car in good working order, the Dauterives hope to sell it and move to something more amenable for their large, growing family. Six kids and counting, as Mrs. Dauterive is expecting again."

We drive a little more and spot Mr. Dauterive. Wouldn't you know he'd live in the house with the tall pole in the yard that has the American flag hanging from it.

To my eyes the Falcon is just another hunk of junk in a world full of them, but Larry and Cornell like the car more than I do. Mr. Dauterive opens the hood, and they move in for a look.

"What strikes you right away about this one, June?" Cornell says.

"The engine smells funny."

"Smells funny how?" Larry asks.

"It smells kind of sweet—like coolant, right?"

"Right, like antifreeze." Cornell turns to Mr. Dauterive. "Did you try running the car this morning?"

"Yes, I did. It ran hot, wanted to overheat in no time, white smoke coming out of the exhaust pipe."

Larry says, "Here's what's happening. Your coolant is getting in the cylinder of the engine, and the cylinder's trying to burn it. We'll need to replace the head gasket. It might take the better part of the day, but we have one in the truck and we can get right on it."

Larry comes up to me and lays his hand on my left shoulder, then Cornell comes over and puts his on my right one.

They're proud of me. That's what they're saying without saying it.

Mr. Dauterive wants us to meet his wife and kids before we get started. "Just take a second," he says, and signals for us to follow him.

As we're walking into the house, he removes his hat and holds it under his arm. "Mother, these are the gentlemen I told you about. The Balls? And that's June. Kids, y'all come and introduce yourselves. Practice shaking hands. There you go. Good job."

The mom is a cheerful person whose long box braids are decorated with silver beads. She wears the same kind of comfy clothes that Mama likes, and when she walks up to greet us she keeps one hand on her hip, as if to make sure it doesn't pop out of joint.

"My dad would be so pleased," she says. "He loved that car."

Shaking hands is a huge deal to the kids. You can tell they've put in a lot of time rehearsing. The oldest is a girl of about eight, while the youngest is a baby scooting around in a walker.

Curious George is on the TV, and a dead plant is in the corner. A box fan blows hot air, rattling the plant's dry leaves. I reach to shake the last kid's hand and notice a spot on the linoleum where somebody stepped on a packet of restaurant ketchup and forgot to clean it up.

Mr. Dauterive looks at his watch. "Got about half an hour," he says, "then I have a funeral detail. Can I get y'all something to drink? A juice box? Bottle of water?"

Larry pats his belly. "Nothing, thanks. We had floats at the drive-in. My body's still in shock from all the dairy."

"Y'all need the facilities they're right down the hall there," Mr. Dauterive says.

We all say no, thank you—of course—since that's policy.

One of the little girls is showing me her Merida doll. She has a brush and she wants me to use it to straighten out the tangles in Merida's hair.

"Like this?" I say. And I do it just like how Mama does it at the salon. The only problem is that Merida has wavy hair hanging halfway down her back and brushing alone can't make it straight.

"My mom's a hairdresser," I say to the girl. "I'll tell you what Merida needs. Merida needs a Brazilian Blowout. That would do it."

I keep stroking with the brush, but the girl's heard enough. She grabs Merida and runs crying down the hall.

"That's not on you," Mr. Dauterive says. "That's on that doll." He looks at his wife. "We're just going to be outside a few minutes."

"Bye," the million kids start yelling.

"Bye," we say back to them.

As soon as we're out in the air again, Mr. Dauterive puts his hat back on. He must get worn out, taking it off and putting it on a hundred times a day. There are definitely more little things to being a cop than I knew.

"Y'all mind if I chat with June here for a bit?" Mr. Dauterive says. He's talking to Larry and Cornell, but his eyes are on me. "Just for a bit, then I'm going to have to go."

"No, sir. Not at all," Larry says.

"June, come around with me to the backyard. We got a swing back there."

The swing hangs from the limb of a tree. It's big enough for three people. When Mr. Dauterive sits down the slats creak and the chains groan and for one scary moment I think we're going to crash to the ground.

"June," he says, "I want you to know I'll make every effort to find your dad. But I'll need you to be patient and to stay positive. And your mom's still back home?"

"Yes, sir."

"Wisconsin, right?"

"Right. Sheboygan Falls."

"Got it, Sheboygan Falls. You try to keep her expecting a good outcome, will you? Last thing anybody needs is to stop believing a reunion is possible."

"Yes, sir."

"Did y'all speak to the police about your dad leaving home? Did your mom file a report with them?"

"No, sir."

"So you didn't call them and you didn't file? And why is that?"

"He's left before, though never for this long. Daddy has PTSD."

"So you know about PTSD, do you?"

"I know a lot of soldiers get it. You can start boo-hooing over nothing."

We are quiet for a while. He's in charge of the swinging. He uses his foot on the ground to control how fast and how high we go.

"Did you notice all the pretty pine trees when y'all were driving in?" he says. "It's my bet there are more pines per square foot in central Louisiana than anywhere else in the world. Pine trees like crazy in Pineville."

I consider mentioning the dead possums but then think better of it. I like him and want him to think I'm only seeing the good, since this is where he lives.

"I helped some old boys from my unit get jobs cutting trees down here. They came from all over—New Mexico, Rhode Island, Pennsylvania. I helped them find a house to rent and fed them quite a few nights. Steaks. Fed them steaks. One would come and stay a while and then leave. Then another would show up. I heard about other units working at farms in Texas—hay, sweet potatoes, soybeans. I even heard of one in Colorado where they have a skydiving school. Seven of them, still jumping out of planes like it was Afghanistan."

"Maybe Daddy's at one of those."

"It's possible," Mr. Dauterive says, "so don't you give up, you hear?" He drags his foot and brings us to a stop. "Listen, June, this is the main takeaway I want to leave you with today. It's not that all those soldiers who came to cut trees like it better here, because they don't. But they're not arguing with their loved ones when they're here, and the loved ones aren't having to be scared when the soldier gets in a mood, you understand what I'm saying?"

"Yes, sir."

"None of us wants to hit the road, June. None wants to run away. Don't ever think for a moment that your father wouldn't rather be with you."

Something he just said makes it hard to look at him.

"Yeah, you heard right," he says. "I chased the wherever road, too. Went up to Maine, of all places, and hid out in the North Woods for close to a year. Chopped wood, fished every day. Meanwhile, my family didn't know where I was." He laughs, then is quiet again.

"A soldier has his or her own healing clock," he says, "and can't take things one day at a time like everybody says to. A day is too long, June. You have to break it down into smaller units. One hour at a time. One minute at a time. A second, even, if that's what you need."

From over at the front of the house I hear the car start. It runs for a short time and then stops. And then Mr. Dauterive sniffs the air, maybe for more of that sweetness I smelled earlier.

He stands and smooths out his uniform. "In case you were wondering, June, the reason I knew your name was right here." And he reaches over and touches the red script on my coveralls.

Don't ask me why I do it, but I reach up and grab his finger and squeeze it tight. "Grateful to you for talking to me," I say.

"Sure, son. Grateful to you for listening."

We're at another rest area, it's four o'clock in the morning, and an old geezer comes walking up to us out of the fog.

The fog is so heavy I thought he was an animal at first, a small bear looking for food. Yeah, food like me.

I'm still half-asleep. Just a few minutes ago the cousins wanted a late-night snack, so we pulled off the road. Now we're sitting at a table with a bunch of chips and sandwiches spread out in front of us. My turkey club tastes all right, although I'm not sure about the sweet bread Cornell made it with.

"Good evening, gentlemen," the man says. "Nice night for a picnic, eh?"

Larry aims his flashlight at the guy's face, and the guy squints and lowers his head. I'd put his age at around sixty. Bristly hair and gray whiskers, a walrus mustache, a heavy face with lids sagging over his eyes. Not to be rude, but he's one of those people you smell before you see.

"I'm a traveler," the man says. "I was wondering if I might get a lift."

"A lift to where?" Larry says. He turns off the flashlight.

"Doesn't matter. Wherever you are going."

"No room," Cornell says. "We're three in the cab already, and the back's full. Besides, we got a policy against that."

"No hitchhikers," Larry explains. "Nothing against you personally, friend, but we can't risk it. We don't have time, besides. We have Fords waiting."

"Fords? Why them?"

"We're mechanics," Larry answers. "Fords are what we do. Hey, tell me, you look familiar. Have we met before?"

The man seems to take offense at the question. He steps closer but the whole time he's looking at me. No, take that back. It's my turkey club he's looking at.

"Would you like some grub, mister?" Cornell says.

The man doesn't answer.

"Come sit down," Larry tells him. "Here. Take a load off. Let's be friends." He slides over and makes room, but the old bird isn't having it.

Cornell reaches into a brown paper bag and removes a sandwich wrapped in cellophane. The guy takes it and tears the plastic off and starts eating. He must be starving, because it doesn't seem to bother him when both the turkey and the bacon fall out and the bread breaks into pieces. A tomato slice also drops to the ground, but the old dude doesn't care. No need to clean the dirt off. No need to bless it. Dirt tastes good with tomatoes, and tomatoes with dirt.

Now he's got mayonnaise all over his whiskers. And the whole time he's groaning. He might be half bear, after all.

"What's your name?" I ask him.

He ignores me, even though it looks like he's done with the sandwich.

"My cousin just asked you a question," Larry says. "He was polite about it. Now what's your name, mister?"

"No way I'm saying," the guy says. "You wouldn't like it, and you're three against one. I ain't falling for that."

"Then make one up," Larry says. "Humor us, why don't you?"

The man's spotted one last shred of lettuce on the ground. He reaches for it and puts it in his mouth. "Louis-Joseph Chevrolet," he says.

You don't expect to ever hear that, somebody speaking French at a rest area at four o'clock in the morning. *Lou-ee Show-zeph Shave-row-lay*, is how he said it. His last name is the same as the car company. It makes Cornell and me laugh, but not Larry.

"*Louis-Joseph Chevrolet?*" he says. "So it started with you, did it?" He lunges at the man and tries to grab him by the

131

neck. The man scrambles backward, falls on his rump, hops back up, then takes off running. He moves pretty well for somebody who just ate a triple-decker sandwich and a bunch of dirt. The fog seems even heavier than before, and the man disappears in it.

"*Monsieur Noeud Papillon,*" Larry calls out. *"Ne pensez-vous pas que vous en avez fait assez? Ou allez-vous?"*

When there is no answer, Cornell tells him to try in English, and Larry yells: "Mr. Bow Tie, don't you think you've done enough? Where are you going?"

That doesn't work, either.

Of course, for all I know I could still be in the truck, and I could still be sleeping. I could still have my head on Cornell's arm, and this whole episode could be another dream. Remember when we were starting out and I saw my classmate puckering her lips? Remember how I saw me and Daddy throwing rocks on the beach? This is what happens to you on the road. You can't always tell what's real from what's a dream.

"Your turn, Mrs. McBean," Larry says when we're on our way again.

FIFTEEN

LATER THAT MORNING WE ROLL into a town like none I've ever seen before.

A pile of broken bricks stands next to a building with walls missing, and sheets of plywood cover storefronts. One place burned and was never cleaned up. Other places don't have roofs or windows to keep the weather from pouring in. The wispy fog looks like smoke, which makes it seem like the town's on fire.

There's not a soul on the streets unless you count ours in the old box truck.

Cornell slows in front of an abandoned movie theater with the word *GEM* on a marquee hanging above the sidewalk. "Who can guess when the Gem played its last movie," Larry says, "but the real question might be whether it was in color or black and white?"

Cornell drives a few streets over and wheels up to the curb. At least here some of the buildings look like they're cared for and still being used, but there are long, empty spaces between them where other buildings would've once stood.

Larry finds an address in his notebook and types it into his phone. Our navigator friend starts chattering.

"Where are we?" I say.

"Cairo," they answer, saying it *KAY-ro*.

"Cairo? As in Cairo, Egypt?"

"As in Cairo, *Illinois*," Larry answers. "Over in that direction is where the Ohio River meets the Mississippi River. We're back in the Land of Lincoln, but we're at the southernmost point—way, way down at the bottom. Kentucky's just right over there. And Missouri's down that way."

He takes the map out of the glove box and opens it, then he lowers a finger to an area that's heavily decorated with stars. "If you'll notice, June, we're farther south than many big southern cities like Richmond, Virginia, and Lexington, Kentucky. See them? It's odd to think that we're still in a northern state, when we're so far down south."

"Can we go someplace else? There can't be a cool old Ford here. Somebody must've lied to you."

The cousins seem to like that. They both chuckle and bump my ribs with their elbows.

"Don't be deceived by appearances," Larry says. "Sometimes the gal in the dirty dress is the best dancer at the ball."

We leave downtown and move out to a neighborhood that's in no better shape. It's mostly vacant lots, and where there are houses, more than a few look deserted. "Client Lila McBean,"

Larry says, reading from his notebook. "Describes her situation as desperate but refuses to provide much information beyond the fact that her Ford's a first-generation Thunderbird convertible. Rather insistent on the phone and sometimes abrupt. Calls at all hours. Often refers to time as if she had less of it than everybody else."

The Australian takes us down a maze of roads with tall weeds growing in the cracks. We end up at a two-story house with a green roof and green-and-white-striped metal awnings. I notice how the house leans to one side and how in the yard a pair of rusty iron poles are supporting it. Their job is to keep the whole stack of dominoes from toppling over.

"Help me, help me, somebody help me, please," Cornell whispers.

It's not the first time he's pretended to be psychic. If he's not channeling another dead Ford, it must be the spirit of Cairo that's talking through him now.

We park and get out, and a lady leaves the porch and takes her time coming down the stairs. She's by far our oldest client yet and must be in her mid-eighties, although mid-nineties also seems possible. She's wearing clunky shoes that clap against the pavement. A tropical-looking scarf is wrapped around the top of her head, and glasses hang from a chain around her neck.

"Well, I can't believe it," she says. "Lord knows you made me beg enough. It wasn't right to treat Mrs. McBean that way."

"Nice to meet you at long last," Larry says. He extends a hand. "Larry Ball."

"And I'm his cousin Cornell," Cornell says.

The lady gives them each a nod, then smiles at me. Some people automatically wonder if I've been kidnapped, and she seems to be one of these.

"Mrs. McBean needs to know," she says. "Are you okay, boy?"

"Mrs. McBean? Who is Mrs. McBean?"

"Me," she says. "I'm Mrs. McBean."

"Yes, ma'am. I'm fine. Sorry about that. For a second there I thought you were talking about somebody else."

"No, only me. But when you get as old as I am you do become somebody else. That must've been what happened to Mrs. McBean. And June is short for Junior, I take it?"

"How'd you guess?" She's the first person all summer to connect the two, and I launch into the whole long story about how Henry Junior turned into June.

"Well, I'll be," she says when I'm done. "You think June is bad, try McBean on for size. 'Beans, beans, the magical fruit, the more you eat the more you . . .' Imagine being a schoolteacher and hearing that every time you turned around to write on the blackboard—that and other things, like body sounds I'd best not mention. Okay, let's go, boys. Preston's T-Bird is waiting."

As we follow her along the side of the house, I can hear a dog barking inside and tracking us from the front all the way to the rear corner. "Go to the pound, pick one out. That's how we used to do it before they invented home security. You got yourself some home security, Junior?"

"You mean like an alarm?"

"Correct."

"No, ma'am, we don't."

"What about one of those doorbells with a camera in it?"

"Not that, either."

"Then you have a dog, don't you?"

I shake my head. "Just a lock on the door."

"And a bat? A baseball bat?"

"Yes, ma'am. We have quite a few bats."

"Good boy. You always want at least one."

The backyard isn't so bad. After seeing other areas of the town, I'd been expecting a whole lot worse.

The fog is lifting and morning light filters through the trees and runs in streaks across the grass. If you look past the boundaries of Mrs. McBean's yard, you can see lonely pilings and cement slabs where houses once stood. As far as I can tell, there's only one other house on her side of the street, and it's three doors down—doors that don't exist anymore, mind you.

"There it is," Mrs. McBean says. She exhales longer than she might need to. "Preston's baby. What's left of it, anyway."

The car's covered with a plastic sheet held in place with cinder blocks. The plastic looks like Saran Wrap, only thicker. "Visqueen," Larry says. "Not very durable, unfortunately."

"Mrs. McBean should've changed it more often, I know that, but step up there and look closer. There's a tarp underneath."

The Visqueen hangs past the wheels to the ground. Cornell lifts it up and you can see mold and mildew, black and red dots and smears coloring the heavy cloth blanket.

"Whoa," he says, squeezing his nostrils to block the smell.

A ratty-looking broom lays on the roof, and soggy brown leaves cover the hood. All four tires are flat and full of dry rot, and the wheels are buried in craters of dried mud.

"Moisture," Larry says. "Boy, do I hate it. I wish your cover hadn't extended all the way to the ground, Mrs. McBean. You've created the perfect lab environment for turning metal into rust."

"I didn't know."

"Don't despair, ma'am," Cornell says in a softer, more positive tone. "Let's not jump to conclusions just yet."

I grab the broom and sweep the leaves off, then Larry and Cornell toss the blocks under some overgrown hedges. They return to the car, and Larry stands back and lets Cornell pull off the covers. Cornell does it the way a magician would. He shouts, "*Voilà!*" and jerks the Visqueen and the tarp off in one fluid motion.

The T-Bird is a disaster if I ever saw one, but Larry and Cornell are acting as if they've discovered the most important Ford rattletrap of all time. After an exchange of exploding fist bumps, they start walking around the car, eyes fixed on it, hands held out as if to warm them against a campfire. They must make ten laps this way, and the whole time you get the feeling they're communicating with Henry Ford himself, or maybe even L. C. Ball, the ancestor who started it all.

A third piece of fabric covers the windshield, and it, too, is full of grime. You can see where either bugs or rodents have eaten large sections.

"And what is this, Mrs. McBean?" Cornell says. "Is that a quilt, a homemade quilt?"

"I was in a sewing club. That's a little blanket I made."

"But why did you put it on the windshield, when you had these other covers?"

"There's a law against having too many covers?"

He shakes his head. "No, ma'am."

The car's original color would've been white, but the paint now looks yellow, and its texture reminds me of an alligator hide. The interior is red with white trim.

"It was his dream," Mrs. McBean says. "I remember when he found the ad in the paper. The car was already ten years old. I told him it would live in the shop and we couldn't afford it. He wouldn't listen. Marched right down to the credit union and borrowed the money."

Cornell pops the hood, and as Larry starts to lift it a mouse jumps out and bounces against my leg. I let out a scream and hop around in the grass. It might make me look weak, but who cares? A mouse just jumped on me.

"Come here, boy," Mrs. McBean says. She puts her arms around me and holds my head against her bosom. "All right, now. Settle down. Shhhhh . . ."

It gets better after the hug, and we all have a look at the engine. It's pretty much what you'd expect, if you weren't expecting much. There are animal turds and dirt dauber nests. The nests are all lined up together, like the pipes on a church organ.

The worst thing, though, is what Larry warned about. The engine's covered in rust.

"Things could be worse," Cornell says. "We had one once where the engine was sitting on the ground. The rust couldn't hold it up any longer."

Good old Cornell, keeping things upbeat, while Larry stands there sulking. I try to see what Mrs. McBean makes of all this, but she turns away, as if she can't bear to look any longer.

"Would anyone like something cold to drink?" she says. "Mrs. McBean has sweet tea, Shasta in the can, cherry Kool-Aid?"

"Nothing for me," I say. But Larry and Cornell never do answer. They're already on their backs under the car, shining their flashlights around.

"First day he brought the car home we kissed on the front seat," Mrs. McBean says. "Preston leaned toward me and bumped the shift and accidently put it in reverse. We went backward into the street before he remembered the brakes. He later told a friend it took him so long because he didn't want our kiss to end. I decided to park it after he passed. Couldn't handle the thought of ever driving it again. Surely the car wasn't entirely to blame for what happened, but it hasn't moved since."

She squats and leans forward on her hands, trying to see what Larry and Cornell are doing. She gives up and taps one of Larry's boots. "Let's talk business," she says. "You might as well tell me now and get it over with: How much is this going to run me?"

They squirm out from under the car. Larry turns off his flashlight and slips it in a pocket, and Cornell does the same with his. "Except for new tires, a battery, fluids, and whatever parts we'll need, nothing at all, madam," Larry says.

"Except for . . . ?" She brings a hand up to her mouth. "Well, that is not true—it can't be. What about your time and trouble?"

They stand shoulder to shoulder and look off at something in the distance. I could see them on a poster for Ford, posing like this with halos over their heads.

"Hello?" Mrs. McBean says.

Larry finally speaks up: "We're here to serve, madam, so please don't worry about the money. We're just grateful for the opportunity."

"Y'all won the Powerball, did you? Come on, you can tell me."

"No, madam," Larry answers. "We scrape by like everybody else. Oh, our garage back home does fine—we have three full-time mechanics at last count, not including Cornell and myself—but it's not cheap saving Fords. For some middle-aged men, it's the casino and the horse track that have their attention. For Cornell and me, it's the blue oval."

"It's blue, is it?"

"Yes, madam."

The way she laughs, you can tell she doesn't believe him. "I'm sick," she says. "You just as well know. It's cancer, stage four. Started in my bowels, is what they tell me. That is why I want the car to run again. I want to remember what it was like with Preston, no top, windows down, love songs playing. He used to peel out. I want to peel out again." She pivots and starts back for the house. "Let me know when you change your mind about that cold drink."

SIXTEEN

CORNELL MANEUVERS THE TRUCK into the backyard, the dog still barking like a maniac in the house. Larry stands in the grass and gives directions, guiding him to a spot in the shade.

Mrs. McBean's house has a back porch that's about the same size as the one in front. The only difference between the two is that the one in back has a screen around it to keep bugs out.

"Y'all ready for a break?" she calls from the back door, even though we really haven't started working yet.

She's carrying a bamboo tray with a stack of cups and a pitcher full of brown liquid. She puts the tray on a little table, then goes back inside. When she comes out again, she's carrying a jack-o'-lantern full of candy. "I still buy for Halloween, but nobody but Maggie comes anymore. They stopped long ago."

I cannot believe my great good fortune. It is barely nine o'clock in the morning and she's offering Kit Kat bars.

"Maggie?" one of them says.

"Neighbor down the street. She knows Mrs. McBean would be sad if no one came, so every year she comes and knocks on my door and hollers, 'Trick or treat.' Tells you the kind of person she is right there."

It turns out the brown liquid is root beer made from a concentrate you mix with water. I'm the only one having a cup. Larry and Cornell suck on sunflower seeds instead.

I think I know what bowels are, but I'll need to ask her later what stage four means.

Inside the house, the phone is ringing. Mrs. McBean waves a hand at it. "Ignore that," she says, as if we were trying to decide whether to run in and get it.

Larry's been waiting for her to look at him. "The generator and power tools, madam. They're noisy. You might not be getting much sleep until we finish, unfortunately. My apologies in advance."

Mrs. McBean sips her drink. "Mrs. McBean is up anyway. For a second I was going to ask you not to disturb the neighbors, but then I remembered I don't have any left. Well, I do have Maggie and her grandma, but they're so far down the street it won't bother them any. Junior, go on, boy, grab yourself another peanut butter cup. Mrs. McBean has chocolate almonds in there, too. *Dark* chocolate. Better for you."

144

"Yes, ma'am." Hey, you don't want to insult your host, do you?

That jack-o'-lantern, by the way, is an old-time papier-mâché pumpkin head with a hunk of rope for the handle. It's bigger around than a basketball, which should give you an idea of how much candy it can hold.

"How long is this going to take?" Mrs. McBean says directly, turning from Larry to Cornell and then back to Larry again. "Not that Mrs. McBean doesn't like you boys, but my clock is ticking louder by the second."

"Not long at all, to get the car running again," Cornell says. "Three or four days if things go well."

"Oh, three or four. Mrs. McBean is good with that."

Larry clears his throat. "That's to get it running. If you want cosmetic work, we'll need to farm it out. Oh, we can make patches here and there, but body work isn't our forte. For a complete restoration you're looking at weeks or even months."

"Months? Really?" She shakes her head. "Mrs. McBean doesn't have months."

I can tell my cousins don't like the thought of letting her down. Neither of them says anything.

"Okay, okay, fine if the car doesn't look like it did. Mrs. McBean doesn't look like she did, either. The windshield. What about that? Think you could change it for me? The glass is broken."

"Yes, windshields are within our purview, madam. Not a problem there."

"Good. That's good. Thank you."

"One more point of discussion, madam. We'll need to dig a hole for our privy. Not a big one. Deeper than it will be wide, I should say."

Mrs. McBean doesn't seem concerned. She shrugs. "You think Mrs. McBean doesn't know what a privy hole looks like? Dig it wherever you want. Mrs. McBean grew up on an outdoor loo, so I can appreciate why you like it. When I was little, it was my favorite place to read. *Hitty* and the Emily books. *The Magical Land of Noom*. It was cooler than in the house, and it was wonderful when it rained, the pitter-patter on the roof." She looks at me over the top of her cup as she sips her root beer.

"You like books, don't you, Junior? You like the stories and seeing all the words typed out on the page."

"Sometimes."

"Sometimes? Only sometimes?"

"I've been reading one about a kid named Jody and his horse that's red. It's not any good."

"Take it with you to the privy next time it rains, see if it doesn't get better." She gets up and shuffles to the door, looking even older now than just a minute ago. "Tired suddenly. Forgive her. Mrs. McBean needs to close her eyes."

She reaches up and makes sure her head scarf is on straight, then she disappears into the house.

We take turns digging the hole, then we get the walls up. Next we raise the shower and the tent. The whole time the radio is playing Beatles music, which has me remembering the old van at Faircloth Motors and the night we hit the road.

That can't have been a month and a week ago. It feels like so much longer, when it's not feeling like just now.

The pallets and the clothes piles. A bottle of Lysol to cut the bleach-and-socks smell. An oscillating fan, hanging from one of the ridge poles.

An hour and a half later and we're done.

I step out of the tent and notice Larry standing by the side of the truck. He's gazing up at the word *Ford*.

You can tell he's been waiting for me to finish with my chores. You can also tell he's upset. I use my hand to block the sun, which is blazing now, and it takes a while for me to see what has his attention. The container is covered in dust, and someone's taken his finger and turned *Ford* into the words *Found on road dead*, the letters streaming down. They're hard to see unless you're looking at just the right angle.

"You didn't do this, did you, June?" he asks. Before I can answer, he's walking around to the other side, which has *Fix or repair daily* spelled out in the dust, also at a clumsy slant.

"When could I have done that, cousin Larry?"

"Just messing with you, son. Come on, now. Where's your sense of humor?" He reaches up as high as he can and wipes off the last letters of *repair* and *daily*, so that it reads *rep* and *dai.* "There's no question in my mind who did this," he says. "It was a bow tie, and not just any bow tie." I can see the veins swell in his neck. "*Lou-ee Show-zeph Shave-row-lay*. He's the one who did it—him and no other. Think, June. Think back to earlier this morning. We're at the rest area enjoying our sandwiches. Our visitor doesn't appear until we're almost finished. Why then? *Why?* Because he was busy earlier defacing our truck, using the fog to keep from being seen."

"It's possible, I suppose."

"They're jealous is all. All of them. The sad fact of the matter is there's not a bow tie in this world who wouldn't want to change his stripes if he could. We are who they aspire to be. And every time they almost have my compassion they go and pull a stunt like this one. June, why don't you undo the hose from the shower and drag it over here? You're the master washer. Get rid of this blasphemy before I throw up in the bushes."

I run over to the shower to get the hose, and Mrs. McBean signals to me from the porch.

"Heard that," she says. "Heard every word. They're cuckoo, both of them. But Mr. Larry is starting to scare me. He's a hothead, isn't he?"

It probably wouldn't be wise to answer, so I don't.

Only now do I notice the dog at her feet, and it's hardly the killer I imagined. Rather, it's one of those teacup breeds you see Hollywood people taking into restaurants with them. They sit at the table and everything. Order an appetizer. This one might be a Chihuahua, but I couldn't say for sure without a magnifying glass.

"You would never suspect a dog that size could have such an ungodly bark," I tell Mrs. McBean. "I was expecting something bigger."

"Oh, Moose might be petite, but she can back it up. Don't you worry about that. You can back it up, can't you, Moose?" And just like that the dog goes off, barking like a lunatic.

You'd think she weighed forty pounds instead of four ounces.

Her name would be Moose. I guess it's funny. Back home there's a Great Dane in the neighborhood called Tiny. The only thing tiny about him is how small he makes you feel when he bends down to sniff your armpits.

"She must have large vocal cords," I say.

"Humongous," Mrs. McBean says. "I have to keep the mirrors in the house turned around. If she ever gets a look at herself, I might lose her to a heart attack."

"You never accidentally sit on her?"

"No. Not yet."

The dog must not appreciate this last question. She answers with more barking and starts spinning in circles.

If she doesn't relax soon I might need to change my shorts. Literally.

"Settle down," Mrs. McBean says. "Come on, you. This is Junior. Junior's a Ford man. Only here to help."

It's probably inaccurate to call me a man, even a Ford man,

but I like it. It comes to me that until I left home I was just a kid who couldn't tell you what kind of pickup his father drove. I'd never washed a car. I'd never helped change the oil or a flat or the plugs or wires that a rat ate. The thing about the road, you pick up a little more about yourself with each stop you make, until an old lady on a porch is calling you a name you never imagined you'd be.

"Listen," she says, "if they try to shave your head, let Mrs. McBean know and I will buy you a bus ticket home."

Larry pulls the telescoping ladder out of the back, extends it as far as it'll go, and stands it against the side of the truck. I climb about halfway up and get to work. The dust comes right off, and the offensive words with them.

The whole time I'm scrubbing, he and Cornell are dismembering the T-Bird. I have a laugh wondering what the car must think, even though of course cars can't do that. But you sit out in the yard for most of your life, not bothering anybody and nobody bothering you, and then one day a couple of cue balls from Wisconsin show up and start taking you apart. I don't know if I would like that if I were a car. But who knows? Maybe cars do, especially those that have been left alone for so long they've begun to rot.

Try standing on a tall ladder with a hose shooting water. I can promise it isn't as easy as you might think. This is the kind of thing Mama would be losing her mind about. Watching me climb to the top and step off onto the roof, as I'm doing now, would have her pretending to faint, her mouth gurgling, foam pouring out. But Larry and Cornell don't seem the least concerned.

"Bloody bow ties!" I shout.

They don't get it at first. Then they see me on top of the container. "Bloody bow ties!" they shout back.

Bloody is a curse word in England that I picked up from a movie on TV a while back. What I like about it is you can say it in America and nobody knows you're slipping one past them.

I wish I could tell you there was a nice view from up there, but it's only nice if you like your views three-quarters empty. I can see the house down the street that Mrs. McBean mentioned earlier. Except for one small area in the backyard, it's hidden behind mile-high shrubs. I try to imagine how the neighborhood looked once. I imagine kids playing ball and jumping rope. I imagine joggers jogging and older folks out strolling. I imagine the houses, trees full of flowers, fruit on the bushes. I suddenly feel bad for Mrs. McBean: stage four cancer, her husband dead, hardly any neighbors left, nobody to share the last days of her life with but a dog that really needs to chill.

If it wouldn't confuse everyone and make them think I'd lost it, I'd turn my face to the sky now and shout: "Yeah, you like to pick on me. But what makes you think you can pick on a nice old lady like Mrs. McBean?"

It would definitely put an exclamation point on this moment, but another line starts banging around in my head, and it's that one from *Titanic*, Mama's all-time favorite. "I'm the king of the world!" I yell, slightly embarrassed for not being more original. "King of the world!"

I stop to catch my breath, and a voice comes from somewhere close by: "Not for long, Jack! You die at the end, remember?"

It's a girl. I must've missed her before. She's standing in the small clearing behind the place with the giant shrubs, one narrow shaft of sunlight blasting through the greenery and striking her hair, some of which appears to be pink. It's a moment you can't prepare for. Not knowing how to respond, I shout out a few "Woo-woo-woos!" the way the other Jack did.

It doesn't impress her. She vanishes before I even finish.

Larry and Cornell must not like that movie, either. As soon as I climb down from the ladder, they walk over with a shovel and tell me we need to dig the privy a little bit deeper.

For lunch Cornell fries Natchitoches meat pies on the cookstove in a pan full of peanut oil. I can smell them while I'm digging, and I remember seeing road signs for the city of Natchitoches when we were in Louisiana. These pies look a little like dumplings, with a flaky shell forming a crust around the meat filling. Cornell bought the ones he's cooking at a country store where we stopped for gas. I guess he couldn't wait any longer. Now that I'm smelling them, I can't wait, either. I throw my shovel down and climb up out of the hole.

We sit in the shade and eat the pies along with mounds of

crispy french fries, and Larry and Cornell keep dragging their whiskers in the ketchup on their plates. It is a very unpleasant thing to watch, and I finally get tired of it and go to the tent for my comb. Next I scout around in the truck for shears or electric trimmers. Lord knows they've got everything else in the back, but all I can find are a pair of rusty household scissors.

"Who's first?" I say, as I walk up with my weapon in hand. Neither seems to understand.

"You slap me around with those mops every time we get the speed up; now it looks like you're bleeding. It's disgusting. All that ketchup?"

"How much are you intending to shorten us by?" Cornell says, looking alarmed.

"Two inches. Three at the most. You won't even be able to tell. You'll still have a good foot to play with. Let's be reasonable. It's time to do this."

I tackle Cornell first, and he's eating a pie and dropping crumbs the whole time. His beard hair is thick and coarse, and it's hard to run a comb through it. I'd wet it, but that would make it curl more, so instead I use my fingers to straighten it as well as I can. I set my bottom line with my comb, then I use a simple blunt-cut technique and make my slice. To give him an attractive box shape, I point-cut the sides all the way up to his face.

"Feel better already," Cornell says, teeth still gnashing his pie. "Feel lighter, too. Oh yeah. I must've needed that. Thank you, June."

It's no different with Larry, although he does seem more attached to his whiskers than Cornell did, even the ones with ketchup. "I'm going to miss my little friends," he says when I finish. He's looking down at the hair on the ground. It looks like some Spanish moss fell from a tree and a squirrel came and bled on it.

"Your mom teach you how to do that?" Cornell says. "I bet she did. That is a fine talent to have and a skill to envy. What would we do without you, June?"

The only thing I've ever seen them eat more of than the meat pies is deviled eggs. I mention this, and Larry asks Cornell again about the secret ingredient in his recipe.

"Is it pickle juice?" he says.

"Nope, not it," Cornell says.

"I don't mean sour pickles. I mean the bread-and-butter kind."

"No. Not those, either. Sorry."

"What about confectioner's sugar?"

You can tell Larry thinks he has it, but Cornell says, "Nope, not sugar. Are you kidding? I would never do that to an egg."

I think Mrs. McBean was right when she said Larry was a hothead. His head has become all red and sweaty.

"Tabasco sauce?" he says.

"Not a chance. It's gotten in this country where everything you put in your mouth tastes like Tabasco. People put it on everything. I even saw some Tabasco ice cream once. No way, not in my eggs."

Larry can't seem to take it anymore. He storms off and dives into the tent.

Mrs. McBean, meanwhile, is walking out with another tray, this one holding a coffeepot and some coffee cups. It must be a thing old people do: walk around with trays all the time. Next to the coffee, there's a bowl overflowing with buttery-looking cheese cubes.

"Go on," she says when she sees my face.

One of them must've told her about my problem.

"Listen," she says, addressing Cornell now, "why are you the studio assistant and Mr. Larry gets to be the artist?"

"Well, that would be because I had a dentist's appointment the day he painted the truck."

Satisfied, Mrs. McBean turns and looks at me. "Junior, honey, I was wondering if I could borrow you. Think that would be possible?"

It's not my fault I'm so slow to get up. Was it my idea for her to come outside with cheese cubes?

"Junior?" Mrs. McBean says. "Mrs. McBean just asked you a question: Would you mind helping her in the house?"

"No, ma'am. Not at all. But shouldn't I change first?" I'm not all that dirty, but I am stalling on account of the cheese.

"Finish your snack, then come," she says. "And don't forget the tray."

I wait until she starts walking off before I glance at Cornell. "Your egg recipe," I say. "The secret ingredient isn't butter, is it?"

He doesn't have to answer; his expression lets me know. "*Ding ding ding ding ding ding ding*," he says, sounding just like Larry did the last time I got the question right on their game show.

I keep waiting for Larry to come out of the tent, but all we get from him is a groan, our poor cousin in his moment of agony and defeat.

SEVENTEEN

MOOSE MUST'VE BEEN putting us on earlier. This time when I step up on the porch, she doesn't act as if she wants to eat me. Instead she jumps from Mrs. McBean's lap and runs over and starts dancing on my boots. I think they call that dance the jitterbug. She moves from one boot top to the other.

"Little two-timer," Mrs. McBean says, taking the tray.

Because her hands are occupied, she enters the house backward, which means she pushes the door open with her rear end. I'll say this much: it's much homier inside than you would think from looking at the outside. I smell furniture polish and something baking. An old clock ticks on the wall. Lace doilies cover the chair arms, each one shaped like a spider-web.

I know they're called doilies because Mama has them all over our house.

There's a little box TV over in the corner, and a commercial for life insurance is on.

"Life insurance?" Mrs. McBean says, almost spitting the words. "Who came up with that? They can insure your *life*? How can anybody insure a life? Look, Junior. Look here at Mr. McBean, how handsome he was. He was a newspaperman."

She points to a group of photos on the wall, all from when she and Mr. McBean were young. Mrs. McBean hasn't changed much, except in the pictures she isn't wearing a scarf on her head and she's not as bony. She was a pretty lady, especially for back then. Mr. McBean liked black suits with white shirts and skinny ties.

Next to the photos are a bunch of framed certificates Mr. McBean won for stories he wrote. Next to the certificates is an article, also framed, written by a reporter for one of the Chicago papers. The headline says, JUST DOING HIS JOB. I have a question to ask. It's a tough one, but I really need to know. Mrs. McBean seems ready for it.

"How did he die, ma'am?"

The best thing is, she doesn't hesitate. "This is still hard for me to say, but he was shot. That's right, baby. Preston was shot. In July of 1967, a young Black man, an army private, only nineteen, had died under suspicious circumstances while in police custody. There was an angry response from the Black community, people protesting police brutality, making their voices heard. Next thing you know hundreds of white citizens formed a vigilante group called the White Hats. For the next two years, the White Hats patrolled the town, and they were even deputized by our sheriff. Some of them carried guns and used them to terrorize our Black neighbors. People took to sleeping in their bathtubs, for protection from the bullets." She pauses and sucks in a breath. "It happened exactly fifty years ago. Preston drove up in the T-Bird planning to cover a White Hats rally. It was dark. He parked and took the key out of the ignition. But he never got out of the car. There'd been complaints about his stories, most from people sympathetic to the White Hats who said he'd taken the wrong side, and we'd had some threatening calls at home. But Preston's killer was never arrested, and this deepened the tragedy for those who loved him. For years Mrs. McBean wanted to blame what happened on the T-Bird— you know, if only Preston had driven something less conspicuous. But how could it have been a car's fault? One little bullet, not this big, Junior"—she's showing the size with her thumb and forefinger—"not this big, and our life together was over."

It feels like a long time before she stops looking at me. "Mr. McBean was a hero," I say. "That's what this guy from Chicago says in his column."

"True, he does say that, but you'd never hear it from Mrs. McBean. Ask me, it was the Black people fighting for their rights who were the real heroes, but that is not to take anything away from my husband. Preston went out to do his job that day—a reporter's job often takes courage, it's true—and it cost him his life."

I spend a minute looking at the small photo next to the

newspaper column. It shows Mr. McBean with a smile on his face. "He looks so nice," I say. "What was he like?"

"Preston? Oh, he was just swell—a lot of fun and goofy sometimes, but also very thoughtful and sweet. A nice guy who loved me. I'm going to tell you something, Junior, and don't think I'm crazy, but sometimes I hear the door to the T-Bird closing—I actually hear it. And I wait, even though I know it's just my mind playing tricks. I look toward the door—that door right there. And I wait for him to walk in and ask what's for supper."

You think you have it bad until you see how others have it. I'm still reading when I feel her hand touch mine. "It's his birthday, baby. Preston's? He would be eighty-six today, same age as Mrs. McBean. I baked him a cake. It's why I asked for your help. Would you be so kind as to sing 'Happy Birthday' with Mrs. McBean?"

It's really not as creepy as it sounds, but I wait a few seconds before giving a nod. "I thought I smelled something when we came in," I say.

"Red velvet, his favorite. You can buy mixes at the store, but I still make mine from scratch, fresh everything."

I follow her to the kitchen, where there's a table piled high with mail. I know what bills look like, and that's what all those letters are. The cake is right in the middle. It has white frosting and so many candles she must've gone through two boxes to have enough. She burns half a box of matches

160

lighting them, and the whole time I'm thinking, *We might get the T-Bird running again, but some things will never get fixed.*

Moose climbs up on my boot and whimpers until I take her in my arms. Mrs. McBean lights the last of the candles, and I can feel the heat on my face. In her eyes the eighty-six flames look like one flame.

"One . . . two . . . three," she says, and we start to sing, Moose barking along. We reach the part where you name the person who's having the birthday, and she sings, "Preston" at the same time that I sing, "Mr. McBean."

When it's over we take in deep breaths and blow at the same time. The candles go out one after another.

Sometimes you eat without tasting. Sometimes you talk without saying anything. I hope by asking for seconds I show how much I like the cake. I hope what I share with her, most of it about Daddy and my own situation, doesn't seem small to someone who's been through what she has.

"I should call Mama more, I know. It's not that I don't want to hear about the weather back home or the haircuts she's been doing, but there's never any news about what matters most to me. Sometimes it seems she's already given up on him and moved on."

A quiet comes over the house, and I'm ashamed to say I'm glad when Mrs. McBean's phone begins to ring. She picks it up and listens. I can see her face redden. "I'm sorry, but you'll need to discuss this matter with my head of accounting if he ever returns from lunch," she says, and hangs up.

Before I leave the house she slices some cake for Larry and Cornell. Each one gets a plate with a big piece and some aluminum foil covering it. As I walk outside my legs feel like Jell-O. I wish I hadn't eaten so much. Even more, I wish I hadn't spilled my guts about Mama and Daddy the way I did.

Over in the shade Larry and Cornell are standing at attention by the T-Bird. They've removed the quilt that was covering the windshield, and now they're staring at the glass.

I told you earlier that they look nothing like my dad. But I see him now in their haunted expressions.

The bullet hole is no bigger around than a penny, with cracks radiating from it in all directions. It's right in front of where Mr. McBean would've sat.

Larry brings his phone up to his face and starts reading aloud. It's an account about Cairo and its troubled history, including the death of Private Robert L. Hunt Jr. Larry's voice lowers to a whisper when he reaches the part about the local reporter who was killed.

"Why didn't she tell me?" he says when he finishes reading. "Okay, cousins, let's get on it. June, come here, son. Cornell will show you how to help remove the broken windshield and store it in the truck. And let's be careful to keep the cracks around the hole from running any more than they already have. Careful, cousins. *Careful!* Too rough and those little cracks'll run clear to the edges. I'm going to order a replacement now. Last thing Mrs. McBean needs is to see that hole again."

I hold up the plates. "What about these? It's Mr. McBean's birthday. She baked him a cake."

They look from the windshield to the plates, then back to the house. Mrs. McBean is still inside. "Okay, but let's make it quick," Larry says.

They sit in the grass and eat with their fingers, while I stand next to the T-Bird and stare at the hole.

I'm sitting in the tent later and talking to Mama on Larry's phone, but we're barely talking. No, we are talking, but it's the same old subject, over and over: Why don't I call her more often?

"You're working, and I don't have anything to say," I say. "It's not you, Mama. I hate the phone."

"Just breathe, then, baby. Let me hear you breathing." She's eating something crunchy. I keep hearing explosions, and I can picture her teeth. You'd think they have diamond bits on the points the way she can cut into hard objects. "It's a caramel rice cake," she says. "My new favorite thing."

"Your chocolate-covered raisins will be jealous when they find out."

"Yes, and let them be. Little rascals." There's no crunching now, no nothing. "When you and your dad were out on the porch all those times," she says, "did he ever say anything about me? Like it was my fault he was so unhappy?"

"Your fault? How was it your fault?"

"I don't know. Maybe . . . Oh, June, maybe I could've been better to him."

"That's not why he left. Get that out of your head. You were always good to him. Nobody could've been better. Come on, Mama."

She's not bawling the way she usually does, but she does start to cry, and I can hear tissues being pulled from a box. "Okay, June, I won't force you anymore, but will you call if you need me or if anything exciting happens?"

"By exciting, do you mean those trees with holes in them? I keep looking, but we still haven't seen any."

"As long as you're looking, that's what counts. Love you, June. Love you with all my heart."

"I love you, too, Mama. Hey, do me a favor, please. Save me some of those rice cakes, will you?"

Classic Mama, she takes another loud bite, then ends the call.

The portable sink we use for cleaning screws and bolts is about the size of a toy wagon though three times as deep. It has a hose on top that dispenses mineral spirits. You let the screws and bolts soak in a bath of the spirits, then you take a small metal brush and scrub the moistened gunk off. The gunk is mainly rust and old deposits of oil and dirt. There's a drum under the sink that catches the dirty spirits that run down a drain. Once this drum fills up, Larry and Cornell drop it off at a hazardous-waste collection site. Cleaning screws and bolts is a real pain.

In my opinion it's worse than taking the carburetor apart and putting it back together again. I wear thick rubber gloves that keep the brush from chewing up my hands and fingernails, and I wear a face mask to keep from inhaling the fumes.

The screws and bolts are the small stuff we have to clean. In a larger sink, Larry and Cornell work on bigger parts like the engine's cylinder heads. There's so much rust on those things that they have to use a power tool with a brush attachment to get it off. The noise rattles your teeth and gives you an instant migraine.

I go at the screws and bolts as long as I can, which is until my fingers start to cramp and my biceps are so sore I can barely bend my arms.

"Dinner tonight is at seven," Cornell says between turns with the electric brush. "A cheese board, to start. Yeah, I thought you'd like that. Then cherry tomatoes sprinkled with vinaigrette. Then we'll have ham steaks, grilled asparagus, and Texas toast with garlic butter. Look, why don't you clean up now, then walk over and invite Mrs. McBean to join us?"

After the shower I go in the tent and sit under the fan trying to cool off. The air's warm, but it still feels good when the blades swing in my direction. I take my time changing. My hair's gotten long since we left Sheboygan Falls. It reaches past my neck. I could cut it myself, but I decide to wait and let Mama have the honor when we get home. I want her to see me with long hair, but even more I want to feel her magic fingers when she's giving me a shampoo in the bowl.

Mama really is talented. She has clients who hug her when they show up for appointments. They surprise her with gift cards even when it's not Christmas or her birthday, and they give her Hallmark cards with notes inside saying how much she means to them. They love how pretty she makes them look, but they love how she makes them feel even more. It's Daddy's fault what happened to us, not hers. Don't think I don't know that.

Through the tent door I can hear the radio playing violin music. It's taped to the side of a tree and they have the volume turned down. I can see Cornell in his *ALEXA* apron. He's pouring a brown liquid into a bowl. Not far from him Larry is lounging in his *Artist* chair and drawing in a notebook.

I like this life, and I understand why they live it. Still and all, I'm missing home, and something in me needs one of Mama's hugs. Without her around I have only my cousins, and I run out now and throw my arms around them—Larry first, then Cornell. They seem confused, but then they're laughing and patting me on the back.

"June," they're saying. "*June!*"

Sometimes I wish I didn't feel so much.

Moose starts yapping even before I reach the porch. Unlike when we first met, it is now a happy yap that says, in human words, "Welcome back, friend. I have missed your delightful company."

The screen keeps me from seeing who's on the porch. I nudge the door open, and it's Mrs. McBean and the girl from down the street.

She's probably just a year older than me, but she's mature in a way that I can't explain. It isn't her clothes, either. She's wearing a *Part Unicorn* T-shirt and black running shorts, and her sponge sandals are shining with fake diamonds. It turns out only a small part of her hair is pink—the inch-wide streak on one side. The rest is dirty blond.

"Hi, Jack," she says, and looks at me as if we have a secret.

"Jack? This isn't Jack. Where'd you get that?" Mrs. McBean waves me deeper inside. "Maggie Moore, meet Junior Ball. Junior Ball, meet Maggie Moore. Junior's from Wisconsin, aren't you, Junior?"

Maggie's been eating a slice of Mr. McBean's cake, and she has to put her fork down. We shake hands and some of the frosting ends up on my fingers, not that I'm complaining. "Are those two baldies really your uncles?" she says.

"Cousins."

"Uncles, cousins. Close enough. Well, Jack Ball from Wherever, Wisconsin, welcome to Cairo, Illinois."

I've never been great at meeting people. The problem is always what to say after you get past hello. "Delighted to be here," I tell her.

"I notice they don't need to communicate when they're working." She's looking past me to our campsite. "The bigger one can touch his nose, and the smaller one knows what to do. If it's the right nostril, it's one job. If it's the left, it's another. They're two halves of a whole, aren't they?"

"I thought so, too, when I first met them, but not anymore. They really are different people."

She stands, and I have to look up a little, and without meaning to I come up onto the balls of my feet. My body seems to do this without permission.

"Your cake for Mr. McBean," Maggie says to Mrs. McBean. "I don't know how you do it, but it seems to get better every year."

"Thank you, sweetheart."

"Jack, Granny and I have over a thousand cable channels and Xbox if you ever need a fix. Come over anytime."

She carries her dirty plate into the house. When she comes back, she's drying her hands on a paper towel. "King of the world," she says with a smirk. Then she walks around the side of the house until I can't see her anymore.

"A person can't have enough friends," Mrs. McBean says.

I'm not sure what to say to that, so I don't say anything.

"She's a smart one, that Maggie. Oh, you have no idea. They got her in the gifted program at school. She took the ACT in sixth grade, scored through the roof. But don't let that intimidate you."

"Why would I be intimidated? What's the ACT?"

Her smile grows into one of those that says she doesn't believe me. "Okay, baby, I'll be there. Seven o'clock sharp."

I was so busy talking I forgot to invite her to dinner. How did she know?

"Oh, nothing gets past Mrs. McBean," she says before I can ask.

Mrs. McBean shows up right on time. She's wearing white pants and a white top, and her head scarf looks more like a turban, with an emerald brooch pinned to the front. She's also put on makeup, and her lips are redder and shinier than before. She looks like one of those people who studies the wrinkles in your palm and tells you how many kids you're going to have. She clutches Moose against her left side like a football she doesn't want to fumble.

The T-Bird is awaiting her inspection. I say this knowing it isn't true—cars are just things; they don't wait the way we do—but this one really does seem alive. In the light from the gas lantern the new windshield reflects Mrs. McBean's face as she stands under the trees, staring at it.

I wonder what she must be thinking. Moose whimpers and glances at me as if for help. Then Mrs. McBean puts her hand on her chest, right over her heart.

First, she looks at Larry and Cornell, eyes moving from one to the other. Then it's my turn. She might settle on me the longest. "Y'all can't possibly know what this means to Mrs. McBean. No, you can't possibly."

They don't say anything, and neither do I, but I'm having

a feeling about myself that I've never had before. It's one I wish would never go away.

I slide over and put my hand on her elbow. Then I guide her to the director's chairs. She sets Moose down on the one that says *Studio Assistant* and she takes the other one.

"Ford men," she says, shaking her head. "Y'all are some characters. I never knew such characters."

I get us some water and wrap the bottles with paper towels. The smell of the food climbs in a cloud and has Moose standing up and dancing, her little nails clicking on the arm of the chair.

"She eat people food, Mrs. McBean?" Cornell says.

"Sure, why not? Since it's a special occasion."

He forks a piece of ham onto a small plate and puts it on the ground. Moose hops down from the chair and comes running over.

"Spoiled rotten," Mrs. McBean says, sounding proud.

I was wondering if one of the chairs might be for Maggie, but it's fine by me if our only guests are Moose and Mrs. McBean. It's hard not to like someone who keeps throwing me the kind of looks they do.

"Time for the entertainment," Larry says. And he and Cornell stand in front of us and clap their hands at the same time. It's just that one clap but you get the message: *Pay attention.*

Larry says, "Ladies and gentleman . . . Cornell Ball!" And Cornell starts walking on his hands, brushing up against us as he maneuvers around the cookstove and between the chairs.

170

He motors out into the yard and cuts between the shower and the thunderbox. He does two full laps around the truck before accidentally hooking a foot on Mrs. McBean's clothesline and crashing facedown.

"Let's hear it for Cornell," Larry says. "Cornell Ball!"

Mrs. McBean likes it so much she gives him a standing ovation. I add a loud whistle, not wanting him to think I didn't appreciate his performance as much as she did.

"Ladies and gentleman, the one, the only . . . Larry Ball!" Cornell says.

Larry sits in front of us and signals for quiet with a finger to his lips. Even Moose stops her nervous dancing. We wait, listening, and after a few seconds I hear something. It's small and far away, but I'm pretty sure it's a cricket's chirp, coming from Larry's mouth.

I couldn't tell you how he does it, but he might be clucking and whistling at the same time, which really does require talent. It's so close to the real thing you wonder if he has a pet cricket hiding in his coveralls.

The most incredible thing about Larry's act might be that he can sing campfire songs as a cricket. The first he does is "The Ants Go Marching." The second is "There's a Hole in the Bucket."

When he starts on "This Land Is Your Land," Mrs. McBean and I sing along, and Moose adds a howl.

"Let's hear it for Larry," Cornell says. "Larry! Larry Ball!" And it's Larry's turn to hear how great we think he is.

It doesn't stop until Moose gets so excited she pees all over Cornell's chair.

We eat in the lantern light, my talented cousins telling stories about interesting Fords they encountered over the years.

Larry remembers a '53 Crestline that a guy from Gaithersburg, Maryland, drove sixty miles each day to and from the nursing home where his wife was living. Years before, when they were young, the man had taken the wife to the drive-in movie in the car. They'd gone to church in it. When their babies were born, they'd taken them home from the hospital in it. A Crestline, squeaky and beat-up. And when the car broke down one day, the man called Larry and Cornell, saying that without his wheels he couldn't visit his wife, and without those visits neither of them was going to make it. Larry and Cornell showed up and got the car running again.

Then Cornell tells about the '56 Parklane that a gal from Sioux City, Iowa, drove on a paper route that started the same year Ford made the car. People in Sioux City grew up with their papers slapping their driveways at the same time every morning. When the slapping stopped they poured out of their homes in pajamas and nightgowns and stared out at the road.

"Where is she?" they said. And somehow they knew that without her their lives would never be the same. So Larry and Cornell drove all night to get to that one. And when they had fixed her car, Sioux City went back to being Sioux City again. And Iowa to Iowa. And America to America. And the world to the world.

Next is Mrs. McBean's turn. "I'm sorry I can't talk about Fords," she says, "but after the T-Bird and what happened to Preston I quit paying attention to cars."

She worked as a substitute teacher in the local public schools for forty-one years, she says. Some years brought in more money than others, but none paid her as much as a full-time teacher or gave her benefits like health insurance and a retirement savings plan. Even though she never had any children of her own, she loved kids and worked hard to teach them. Other substitutes were nothing more than babysitters. When she had a job at the high school, she hitched a ride with Mrs. Thompson, the science teacher. Then after Mr. and Mrs. Thompson moved to Omaha, Mr. Odom came to get her. She rode with him the longest. He was a bachelor, taught typing. A very shy man. He owned five suits. On Monday he wore the Monday suit, on Tuesday the one for Tuesday, and on and on. The day he retired, Mrs. McBean got out of his car and she could tell there was something he wanted to say. She waited, leaning in, an uncertain smile on her face.

"Thank you for understanding, Mrs. McBean," he finally said.

She whispered, "You're welcome, Mr. Odom." She closed the door, and he drove off.

"Thank you for understanding what?" Larry says.

"He didn't say."

"About his suits maybe?" I say.

She shrugs. "Could be. But I always wondered if it was

why he never stopped on the drive home and bought me a coffee."

We need a long time to think about that one. Larry and Cornell give up and start eating again. They hold their asparagus with oily fingers and make each spear vanish with little barracuda bites. Mrs. McBean, meanwhile, eats without appetite, the ham barely rating a nibble. Eventually she puts her plate away.

"I feel guilty just telling that story," she says. "Like I was stepping out on Preston."

"Oh, no," both Larry and Cornell say.

"Which I never did."

"No. Not you, madam."

"Okay, Junior," Mrs. McBean says. "The stage is yours, but no pressure."

Shoot, I think. *Shoot!*

I have to tell them something, something where there's a car in it, so I go with the one about finding Daddy asleep in his pickup. It was early in the morning and freezing outside, but when I pulled the door open warm air spilled out. He'd been lying on his side across the seat, balled up like a shrimp. Nuttiest of all, he was wearing his army uniform, the dress one with all his medals and the khaki beret. When I asked him why he was dressed that way, he said he couldn't remember. When I asked him how he'd kept warm, he said, "Well, by running the heater." He and Mama had had words after I went to bed, and he thought he'd show her by staying outside all night. As it got colder, he'd gotten in the pickup.

"She saved me," he said, meaning the truck.

I helped him in the house and led him to their room. Mama was still in bed, facing the wall. She didn't say anything, but I noticed her eyes were open. He took the uniform off and hung it in the back of the closet, then he got under the covers as if nothing had happened.

Not that I was expecting applause, but the response is even worse than what Mrs. McBean got. Everybody is silent when I finish. And this silence goes on for a while, until finally a cricket saves the day.

It's hard to hear at first, but then it gets louder and louder, clucking and whistling both at once.

We automatically turn to Larry, even though it can't be him. Done with dinner, he's stuffing sunflower seeds into his mouth. And so we know it's a real cricket, off somewhere in the darkness, reminding us we aren't alone.

EIGHTEEN

THE NEXT MORNING MRS. McBEAN arranges liquid refreshments in a washtub on the back porch. Pretty bottles bob in the ice melt, along with soft drinks in cans and a large jug of raspberry tea. "It's the same tub I bathe Moose in," she says. "Don't worry. I cleaned it good."

If anybody has a sweet tooth, there are little squares of Mr. McBean's cake that you can eat with a toothpick. There are also store-bought banana crème cookies and banana moon pies. Mrs. McBean is a broken record when it comes to bananas. She also has some real ones.

Because of our dinner party, Larry and Cornell let me sleep late. I lean back in one of the porch chairs and let out a groan. "You want Mrs. McBean to fry you an egg?" she says.

"No, ma'am. No eggs."

"Then have a banana." But that doesn't sound good, either. I groan again and Mrs. McBean says, "All right, I hear you. But at least you weren't up all night. They didn't have a wink between them. I know this because I was up, too. They broke for coffee at around three and said they might need to have another part FedExed. Mrs. McBean told them she would pay for it. They said no, it was on the house. Then Cornell disappeared and came back a while later with the part they needed. It was a fan, about yay big. He'd made it from pieces of scrap metal they had in the back of the truck."

"Uh-huh," I say.

"'Uh-huh'? Oh, Mrs. McBean doesn't respond to *uh-huh*, Junior. If a child said that in my classroom, she would make him stand in the back with his nose pressed into the corner."

I carry Moose with me to the other side of the porch and stand in the corner with my nose pressed against the place where the walls meet. "Like this?"

"Boy, you are humorous. No wonder all the girls are crazy about you."

I take it she's talking about my budding love affair with Moose, but when I return to my chair she hands me an envelope sealed with penguin stickers. "If you weren't such a sleepyhead, she could've given it to you herself."

Mrs. McBean is aware of my sudden need for privacy. I start for the tent, but she says "No," and holds her hands out for Moose. They retreat into the house, Moose not happy about it.

I flop back in the chair and open the letter.

Dear Jack,

Here is an invitation to join me for a bike ride and a picnic. Since you and your cousins won't be staying long, we should have our adventure ASAP, don't you think? You can borrow Granny's bike. It doesn't have a crossbar but so what? You seem confident enough to handle it, and no one will see us, besides.

> *Walk over when you're ready,*
>
> *Maggie*

I force myself to eat a banana. Then I eat a second one. Bananas are supposed to be brain food. If I hope to keep up with somebody who scored through the roof on the ACT, whatever that is, I might be wise to eat the entire bunch.

And so I do.

Larry and Cornell are cool about it. They're changing wheel bolts with a propane torch, anyway, and it's a job I'm not skilled enough yet to help with. They've elevated one side of the car with jack stands, giving them room underneath to root around.

"Oh, just remembered," Larry says, wiping his face with a shop cloth. "I had a call last night from our next stop. It's urgent, I'm afraid, which means we'll be needing to hit the road soon. You go and have fun. It might be your last opportunity. If all goes as planned, we'll be leaving in the next day or two."

"Seriously? We just got here. And there's no way this car will be ready." It is a lame protest, but at least I'm loud while making it.

"Our assignment is to get the T-Bird running again," Larry says, "not to restore it to its original condition. This is a hard lesson, and it never gets any easier, but we take our friends with us, June, even when we have to leave them behind. That might be the worst part of our job. It's also the best."

I change out of the coveralls and into clean clothes. I brush my teeth with a bottle of water, then I climb into the back of the truck and comb my hair in the mirrors hanging from the ceiling. Fifty June Balls are looking back at me, one as terrifying as the next.

"I told her to show you our pretty library, but she wants you to see Fort Defiance," Mrs. McBean says. "That's the park where the two big rivers come together. They meet right there at a place called the Point. It's also where Preston and I used to go to make out. Spread out a blanket, have some wine, some little mint cookies. In *Huckleberry Finn*, Huck and Jim are trying to get to Cairo on their raft, but they get separated in the fog and go right by it. You ever hear of Huck and Jim, baby?"

"Not sure. I might have."

"Huck was the boy, Jim was the slave who ran away. They went down the Mississippi River. If they could ever reach Cairo, they could get on a steamboat and go up the Ohio River to the North and the free states, where Jim would be free and all his problems over with. On our picnics, Preston used to pretend to see them floating by, Jim still on the raft, Huck chasing behind him in a canoe. 'Huck! Jim!

Turn around! Turn around!' I swear Mrs. McBean laughed so hard she almost peed her pants, but now that I think about it, maybe it isn't so funny. Jim couldn't be free if they kept going, could he, baby? He stayed a slave instead." She looks at me. "I talk too much."

"No, ma'am" is all I can think to tell her.

"I was too in love. That happens. I saw only us, nobody else, not even the man on the raft trying to be free."

Maggie's grandmother isn't at all what I was expecting. Her hair isn't even gray. She has a long, layered shag with highlights, a look that's just right for her moon-pie face. And she's wearing stretch shorts and a *PINK* shirt. Best of all, when she answers the door she's eating a bag of candy.

"How goes it, Jack?" she says, and offers me a smile full of Sour Patch Kids.

Her bike is a Schwinn from when she was a kid, which would make it about fifty years old. It's white with red stripes—the same general color scheme as the T-Bird. There's a headlight on top of the front fender, and the seat is decorated with a large letter *S*.

Maggie and I roll the bikes out of a storage room and check the air in the tires. She must've oiled the chains earlier because they're dripping. Hers is a Raleigh with a basket on the handlebars that's holding things for our picnic: food and water and a blanket and half a roll of paper towels.

"When your stay in Cairo is over, Jack," Maggie's

grandmother says, "please remember to say good things about us. I can assure you there's more to the town than our tragic past and all we've lost. The people can be pretty great—I hope you get to meet more than just us. I also hope you notice the old homes that have been lovingly restored and overlook the dilapidated ones. Take this place, for instance. Yes, my gardening leaves much to be desired, but isn't the house itself absolutely charming? It's a Sears house. Ever hear of Sears houses?"

"Sears like the store? Like what used to be at the mall?"

"Yes, one and the same. A hundred years ago the company shipped house kits with precut lumber from right here in Cairo. Nowadays we think we're so special because we can order groceries from Amazon, but back then you could buy a whole house from a catalog and have it delivered." She pauses and makes her eyebrows dance. "In my humble opinion, the latter is more impressive than the former."

I always get mixed up over my latters and my formers, but I get what she's saying.

She's saying the internet really isn't so great.

"Save some of those for me, will you?" Maggie says to her grandmother, meaning the candy. In the next second she's riding away.

Her bike is a lot faster than mine, or maybe it's just that I'm slower at making mine go. We ride up and down streets that are mostly empty.

Maggie must notice my reaction. She slows down and

sort of announces: "The black windows of the old houses gaze out at the world with the same sad question: *Why?*"

"Huh?" I say.

"No, not *huh? Why?* The question is *why?* Why have so many people abandoned us? Why don't they come back?"

I'm so busy taking in the passing scenery that I don't notice when she pulls off the road.

"Here," she says, as I go riding past.

Her bike is lying in the grass, and she's sitting on the porch of a house with holes in it: holes in the roof, holes in the chimney, holes in the walls. Vines that might be poison ivy cling to the window screens. You feel as if you could break out in a rash just looking at the place.

Maggie's legs are swinging back and forth, her feet barely missing the ground.

"Are we trespassing?" I ask, and point to the sign by the door warning against it.

"Are we?" She pats the place on the boards next to her. "This is my old house, Jack. It's where we lived when I was little."

"Here?" As I fall back next to her I rap my knuckles against the porch boards. "No way."

"It's another Sears house. My mom loved her Sears house, just like Granny. See that mailbox over there? It used to have our name on it."

The box is in the weeds, smashed to pieces. There are a few letters and a number on the side, but they don't spell out anything that you can read—no name, no address. Someone must've used the box for batting practice.

"Granny doesn't approve, but I like to come and check on my room every now and then. It's upstairs. Would you like to see it?"

She doesn't wait for an answer. I get up and follow her in, the door squalling on rusty hinges.

"If I were an escaped convict looking to hide," I say, "this would be the perfect place."

"Hey, can we agree about something? Since this is still technically my house, please talk nice about it or say nothing at all. You live in Cairo, you get tired of the negative comments."

I lower my head. "Sorry."

The first room, which was probably the living room, has trash on the floor, most of it empty beer cans and tins for foods like Vienna sausages and potted meat. My dad was always eating weird stuff like that, and for one ridiculous moment I actually wonder if he's responsible for the mess. Could he have camped here between one stop and another? It might be how a little kid thinks, but you need to know where my head is. There's a corduroy shirt on the floor, and somebody left a shoe behind. I pick them both up for a closer inspection.

Nah, too small.

"The couch was here," Maggie says. "We had a coffee table made from an old door. It was here. My mom sewed all the curtains herself with material from the Walmart in Sikeston.

We had a mailman, Mr. Lee, who used to talk to my dad about sports. On Sundays we'd have chicken wings. Yummy, Jack. *Yummy!*"

I'm not sure what to add about the chicken wings, but I know it's not another *yummy*. I just smile at her instead.

"You dip them in ranch dressing. Can't forget the ranch."

I follow her up the stairs, which are also a disaster. The carpet's rotten and it stinks. Halfway up there's a spot where it looks like an animal died. To step over it you need to hold the railing, and you need to take two steps instead of one.

I wish the stairs didn't creak so much. I'm already freaked out enough.

We come to a landing that connects with a short hallway. There are several doors on either side, all but one open, and that is the door she chooses—the closed one. She turns the knob and pushes it open, and before she steps inside she turns to face me. "I never had a boy visit my room before. Good thing for all concerned we're just friends."

The room is a shock, after what I saw in the rest of the house. It's spotless is why. And it looks like somebody came in and cleaned this very day. I can smell Clorox. I can see the floor shine.

In other parts of the house it looked like water flowed in from the ceiling, but this room doesn't have that problem. I look everywhere, and there's no mold growing on the walls.

"I know you've been wondering, so let me just come right

out and say it." She takes in a deep breath. "I live with Granny because they left, too, only their problem wasn't the war, it was drugs. And it's still their problem, as far as I know. Have you ever heard of meth, Jack?" She turns her back to me as soon as she asks the question. That tells me not to say anything.

"My bed was here," she says. "I had a Katy Perry poster here. When my dad cut the grass, I would sit at the window and watch him. Before it got bad he was so handsome, Jack. Oh my God. Do you want to picnic here or do you want to go to the Point?"

"Mrs. McBean said the Point is a long way away."

"To a hundred-year-old lady it might be. Not to us." Before I can make a choice she says, "That wasn't right. What I just said about Mrs. McBean? What is wrong with me, adding the years like that?" She opens a window and sticks her head out. "Forgive me, Mrs. McBean. You know I love you."

Even though Mrs. McBean lives five blocks away.

"It's nice in here," I tell her. "I like it. It's twice as big as my room back home, and it smells better."

"Thank you. Thank you so much. Mom used to scold me when I wouldn't pick up. It's ready now, don't you think? For when they come back?"

I stare at her across the room, trying to figure out if she means it. The obvious reply would be, "You really think there's a chance they'll come back?" but I can see she needs a different answer, so I say, "Yes, I do."

"Mrs. McBean told me about your dad, Jack."

"Yeah? You two were talking about me?"

"Only good things, I swear. Like how polite and friendly you are. Do you think he'll ever come home? Your dad, I mean?"

"I'm counting on it, Maggie. He never seemed like the kind of guy who was faking it—faking the father thing, you know? Something must've happened."

"Like he got kidnapped?"

"I thought of that."

"Or fell in a hole. He was out walking and there was a hole and he fell right in. Nobody's found him yet, but one day they will."

I'd rather somebody kidnapped him. If he fell in a hole, how would he eat? How would he drink unless it rained? After months by himself down in the hole, how would he find the strength to climb out?

I don't want him to be in a hole.

"That's how I used to think about my mom and dad—kidnapped, fell in a hole, took a plane somewhere and can't come back because they ran out of money. Have amnesia and spend their days roaming the earth trying to remember who they are. We have a lot in common, don't we, Jack?"

She's looking around the room, her eyes following a path up the walls to the ceiling and to windows where you can see outside to the treetops.

"He grilled them on a hibachi," she says. "Those chicken wings? Sometimes I can still taste them, I don't know why."

186

What can I do to make things better for this kid? How can I help her?

These questions make me sound more like Larry and Cornell Ball than June Ball, but they're in my head as we ride to the Point. I can feel the heat in my lungs when I inhale, and I can feel a small burn in my nostrils when I exhale. I'm grateful when we break for water. I'm a sweaty pig.

"Almost there," Maggie says.

I nod even though my insides are melting. I bet I look bad: hair dripping, red splotches on my face.

Oh well. What can you do?

"I've been wondering," she says. "How do you and your cousins keep your outfits clean?"

"You mean our coveralls?"

"Is that what they're called? Okay, then. Your coveralls."

"Sometimes we just wash them with a hose and some soap out in the yard and hang them in the sun to dry. Other times, if we're going to be in a town a while, we go to a Laundromat or leave them with the cleaners."

She takes a long sip from her water bottle, then puts it back in the basket. I drink all of mine and can't decide what to do with the empty. We're so far out in the sticks nobody would care if I threw it in the grass, but it comes to me that Cairo deserves better. It's had enough people dumping trash wherever they felt like it.

"I hear you're a real cheese freak," Maggie says. "So guess

what? I brought a family-size bag of Cheetos, just for you."
She reaches for my empty and puts it in the basket next to her
bottle. "You don't have many friends, do you, Jack?"

"Not many," I say, wondering what gave it away.

"I don't, either. So don't feel bad about it. If I had to
define our relationship I would say we're more like siblings
than friends."

By siblings she means brother and sister. I know that much.

She smiles and says, "The black windows gaze out at the
world with the same sad question. And what is that question,
Jack?"

"Why?" I say.

"*Why?*" she answers.

We get up on our bikes and start pedaling again, and I say
what I have to before she can pull out too far ahead: "Hey,
listen. Hey, Maggie? I wanted to tell you something. I never
liked my name. I look in the mirror and it's not June looking
back. It's not Henry or Junior, either."

"I guess not. Because you're Jack."

"Yes. But I didn't know it until Cairo—until you told me."

"You're welcome," she says, having to shout because of
the wind in her face. "If what you're trying to do is thank me."

We enter the park and pedal down to where the land ends and
the rivers meet. It feels like we'll never get there. "See now
why they call it the Point?" Maggie says. "Awesome, ain't it?

The Mississippi's a lot muddier than the Ohio. I saw some video of it from a drone and one side's chocolate brown and the other's crystal clear."

There are a few cars parked in the parking area and people standing on an observation deck, one of them videoing the water with her phone. Nobody's picnicking, and nobody's as young as we are. Looking at a place where there's a lot of water must not be very exciting for most kids.

I help Maggie lay out the blanket then we unload the basket with the food. She hands me the bag of Cheetos, and I crack it open and get busy doing what I do best.

In the sunlight the pink streak in her hair looks almost orange. "Is that an extension you clipped in or had bonded?"

"You're a boy, Jack. What can you possibly know about it?"

"Or maybe it's a dye job over bleach. No? Not that? Then it's sticker hair—what Mama calls sticker hair. Everybody else calls them tape-ins."

"A boy," she says again. "A boy who knows all about Fords and all about hair, too? Gosh, Jack, what kind of boy are you?"

"Just one whose mom works in a salon."

When she smiles I know I'm safe. She reaches over and takes one of my Cheetos. She takes it out of my hand, not out of the bag.

"Granny says two people died that day: Mr. McBean and then Mrs. McBean. It's why she stayed in Cairo—she couldn't leave him. A lot of people tried to get her to move, like the

friend who showed up with a U-Haul, but she always said no."
She steals the last of my Cheetos and bites into it. "Ready for
your sandwich, Jack?" And she hands me one.

I suppose I could stand and point at the water and pretend
to see Huck and Jim, but I'm not feeling it.

"I promised Granny I'd be back by three," Maggie says
when we're done eating, "so it's time now."

It's a relief, to be honest. I was running out of things to
talk about, and I didn't think I could say the word *why* again
without having to scream first.

We put everything in her basket and have one last moment
with the water. It's too bad Huck and Jim passed by Cairo in
the fog, but you have to blame the writer, whoever wrote that
book. He could've made it a sunny day.

If he were to tell my story, you can bet I'd never find my
dad. In the end the writer wouldn't let me. Just how some
people are, I guess.

"Is it fun being a boy?" Maggie says.

"It's pretty good. What about being a girl?"

"I like it most of the time. Come on, Jack. You take the
lead riding home. I don't mind."

It's been about an hour since we returned from the park, and
this time when I go to Maggie's old house I go by myself. And I
walk. I'm carrying a rake in one hand and a box of garbage bags
in the other. I also have some work gloves in my back pocket.
Larry and Cornell keep all these things in the truck, and when

I asked to take them, they said, "Anything you need. *Nuestra casa es su casa.*"

Meaning our house is your house.

Before this summer, would I have ever volunteered to clean a flophouse? No way. I put up a fight every time Mama told me to clean my room. But you finally decide what kind of person you want to be, and then the rest comes down to having the courage to be it.

But no lectures from me.

The job reminds me of when I had to write papers for Mrs. Vicari's language arts class. You start with one sentence that makes sense and isn't full of mistakes, and then you write a second sentence that makes sense and isn't full of mistakes. Then you write a third sentence. Then a fourth. Before long, the assignment's done and you're back on YouTube watching reunion videos.

I push the door open. I'd be lying if I didn't say I automatically feel like puking at the sight.

Start small, I remind myself.

One sentence at a time, one pile at a time.

I finish the first room, then start on the second. The bags are piling up. I drag them outside and find a spot on the side of the house where you can't see them from the street. The third room doesn't take long. Neither does the kitchen. The kitchen's pretty disgusting—what is *that*?!—but I find a rhythm and get it done.

The stairs. Oh, man, the stairs!

No, it isn't a dead animal. It's more like an atomic food bomb went off, splattering spaghetti sauce over everything.

How many sentences have I written now? What about bags—how many have I filled? Go ahead and count them.

I can see it; I can see the end. Won't be long.

For Maggie, I tell myself. *For Maggie, Jack. Do it for Maggie.*

When it's over I lie on the porch and try to will myself to stop sweating. I can see stars twinkling through the trees, which tells me it's getting late. I can hear a bird singing, all by itself, and the wind starts to blow, and a deep peace finds me. Cairo kind of scared me when I first saw it, but now I realize that I wasn't seeing it at all. A dragonfly settles on my leg and looks at me, the beat of its wings keeping time with the beat of my heart. Sometimes you just have to give a place a chance. Same for people. Same for dragonflies. "Hello there," I tell this one. "Would you like to come on the road with me? Help me find my dad?"

It flies off without answering, or maybe that is its answer.

"You're right," I say. "It really is up to him. It always was. Thank you, dragonfly."

I don't want anybody worrying about me, so I gather my things and start back for Mrs. McBean's. My brain has to scream at my legs just to get them to move my feet one in front of the other. There are only two garbage bags left in the box. I hope Larry and Cornell forgive me for that. And I'll need to clean the gunk off the rake tines first chance I get.

Mrs. McBean is sitting on the back porch with Moose, and I'm not prepared for the commotion they make when I walk up. I suspect Mrs. McBean would wrap me up in her arms if I smelled better. As for Moose, it doesn't seem to bother her that her boyfriend reeks. She trembles so hard with excitement she has another accident, this time on me.

"Where on earth have you been, child?" Mrs. McBean says.

"Nowhere."

"Nowhere? Really? That must be where children go right before they get their butts spanked."

"I had something to do."

"Yeah? Well, you still should've told Mrs. McBean first. How was anybody supposed to know you'd be gone five hours. You missed supper, Junior."

Supper . . . how about that? Who says *supper* anymore? You really do have to love Mrs. McBean.

"I'm sorry. Am I too late?"

"No. It's never too late when you're at Mrs. McBean's. But you had me worried to death, boy."

"What is stage four? What is that?" I say it even though I don't really intend to. It just comes out.

"It means when the cancer has spread to other organs in your body."

I take a seat and calculate what to say next. Across the yard Larry and Cornell have turned on the klieg lights, and they're both elbow-deep in the engine. The little radio is playing orchestra music.

"I wish I could make it go away for you," I say.

"Yeah?"

I add the nod she seems to want. "Maybe riding in the T-Bird again will help do that. Peeling out, like you say."

"Maybe so. And all the bad things will go away. All the years. Mrs. McBean will be young again, and she'll still have Preston." She stands and shuffles over to me. "By the way, your cousins had more setbacks—unforeseen difficulties, Mr. Larry called them—so they wouldn't eat my chicken fiesta casserole. Wanted something light. I cut them up a honeydew melon instead. I couldn't interest you in some fiesta casserole, could I, boy?"

She puts her hand on the side of my face. Then she leans over and kisses the top of my head.

"I think you could," I answer.

NINETEEN

THE GAS IS SOUR, and they see red flakes in it when they drain the fuel tank. Red flakes aren't good. They mean the tank has rust.

There isn't a replacement tank in the truck or a source for a new one in town. We could have one shipped overnight, but the more practical option is to take the original tank to a radiator shop and have it lined with a coating to prevent rust and future leaks.

Cornell ends up taking it to a town in Missouri that's nearly an hour away. It costs him the better part of the day.

"You can't ever predict these things," Larry tells me, "except to predict they're going to happen. We'll just keep at it, you and me. All we can do."

He uses a floor jack to lift one side of the T-Bird, making it easier to reach the undercarriage. My job for the afternoon is to scrape off dauber nests. I use putty knives, a steel spatula, and a wire brush. The daubers fly around the car but leave me alone. Larry says they rarely sting humans, the way paper wasps and yellow jackets do. Inside the nests I keep seeing these crunchy things that might be their babies, and it bothers me to have to crush them along with their mud forts. It makes no sense to me why dirt daubers even exist. I mean, what's the point of a stupid dirt dauber? I wonder if they're food for birds, which would make them part of the food chain. Speaking of food, that fiesta casserole last night gets an A plus. Poor dirt daubers. I know they didn't ask for any of this.

I'm down there on my back when Larry slides next to me.

"Old Fords might be my passion," he says, "but I've always had a heart for neglected and forgotten things."

I don't remember asking him about his passion, nor about his heart. Last thing we talked about was dirt daubers. He starts nodding his head.

"I mean Cairo, of course," he says.

"Break time!" Mrs. McBean shouts from the porch.

"It explains my sympathy for the place," Larry continues, not seeming to hear her. "I can't help but root for it—root for a comeback. Did you know the population went from fifteen thousand to less than two thousand in the last one hundred years? And the numbers continue to decline, but Mrs. McBean has stayed and battled on. Years and years, June. And yet more years. Consider what she's made of, to live the life she has and to face the end now with a wish that most people would consider absurd." He runs his hands over his bald head.

"To peel out in her husband's T-Bird," he whispers, as if the idea is still a little peculiar to him, too.

"I think it's kind of . . ." I stop myself.

"Kind of what?"

"I don't know. Kind of beautiful—yeah, that's the word."

He watches me chip away at more nests, these glued to the wheel well. "You and your dad will be together again one day. I'm certain of it."

I don't know why he had to say that, either. But it's good to hear, and it makes me stop working.

"Break time!" Mrs. McBean yells again from the porch.

Larry slides back out and stands up. He waves a wrench at her, letting her know we're coming.

I turn sideways and look up at him from under the car. "I wonder what it'll be like when I do see him again. In the reunion videos they always cry and hug each other and roll around on the ground. I can't see Daddy doing that."

Larry's drying his hands on a shop cloth. "I can," he says. "He only got hard because he had to. Wouldn't have survived otherwise. Sometimes you remind me so much of him I want to call you Henry. I have to catch myself."

"Why did you stop being close?"

"The war, son. We tried all we could, cousin Cornell and me. It wasn't our choice. First summer after you were born, we scheduled some Ford stops in Georgia just to see you. Couldn't get down there fast enough. Henry wasn't sick yet.

I held you in my arms; Cornell held you. And what a fine baby you were. My my. By the time your dad moved you and your mother back to Sheboygan Falls he was someone else. We recored his radiator at the shop, and he came in inebriated and told us to leave him alone. Said it would be better for everyone. The sweet memories of us as boys together put him in a bad way. He told us that. He couldn't square them with the other memories—you know the ones—and the guilt would sneak in and crowd his mind. I don't like it any better than you do, and I still don't completely understand it, but we got to feeling that if we weren't helping him we were part of the problem, so we decided to honor his wish and keep away. Now that was tough, you being a young boy then. I wish we'd known you before now, June, and I know Cornell wishes the same. A first cousin once removed ain't nothing to sneeze at, especially when he's a Ball."

Mrs. McBean is standing at the edge of the porch, the silhouette of her body dark against the silvery screen.

"She wants you, June, not me," Larry says. "It's how God made things, the old always trying to wrap their arms around the new. Go ahead and put your tools down. The daubers have been here fifty years. They can wait a little longer."

I walk over, and she's left the back door open a crack. I take it as an invitation to go inside, and I find her in the kitchen paying bills.

She looks over the top of her reading glasses. "Here, baby. Sit. Mrs. McBean poured you a glass of Kool-Aid."

My coveralls are still dirty from the daubers, but I walk over and put my arms around her anyway.

"Oh, thank you, Junior," she says. "Mrs. McBean can't tell you how nice it is to have a man in the house again."

I sit across from her and sip the cold drink. I'm burning hot and don't think I ever tasted anything so good. "The man I'm named after? This Henry Ford guy?" I wait until she nods. "Cousin Larry told me he said bad things about Jewish people."

"Are you named after Henry Ford? Really? I thought you were named after your father, Henry Ball Sr., and that's why I've been calling you Junior and other people call you June."

"Yes, ma'am, but my dad was named after Henry Ford."

"But not you."

"No, ma'am."

She's looking over her glasses again. "Have you ever heard your dad say bad things about people?"

I shake my head. "Only about himself."

"Only about himself," she repeats. "Listen, Junior, I don't know much about Henry Ford. I'm sorry to learn he entertained such ugly thoughts in his head—there's no excuse for it. But he's been bones in the grave a long time now, and you and your dad are alive and the only Henrys you should be worried about, until you meet another one you might want for a friend." She reaches across the table with her hands, both of them, and I give her mine. "You remember what I said about names when we first met, don't you, baby?"

She must see the smile coming up on my face, because she answers before I do: "Beans, beans, the magical fruit . . ."

It makes me feel better, hearing her laugh. A little later she walks with me out onto the porch. I open the screen door and turn back to look at her one more time. "You be you, baby, whoever that is. Henry. June. Junior. *Jack!* You and you alone. Do you promise Mrs. McBean?"

"I promise," I say. Then I wave goodbye and head out as if I really am going somewhere other than the place under the trees on the other side of her backyard.

Later that night I'm lying on my pallet, and I must fall asleep with Maggie in my head, because I have this dream where we're back at her old house. We're climbing the stairs, and we step over the food bomb and make it to the landing, and her bedroom door swings open.

This is where her bed was. This is where her Katy Perry poster was. Maggie's in a blast of sunlight, and she's looking at me from across the room. And she's about to say, "Sometimes I can still taste them, I don't know why," when the T-Bird starts with a bang and a clatter that shake the ground beneath me.

"Mrs. McBean," I call out, and scramble out of the tent. Then I say it again, even louder: "*Mrs. McBean!*"

I start moving toward Larry and Cornell at the same time Mrs. McBean staggers off the porch and into the grass. She and I come together under the trees and hold each other in the glow of the klieg lights. "*Preston!*" she cries out.

I take her hands in mine and spin her around in a slow circle. If she weren't so fragile, I wouldn't have to be so gentle with her, and we'd be cutting circles all over the yard. She laughs and throws her head back, and her headpiece flies off and lands in the grass. She's balder than I thought, completely bald. I've seen bald ladies at the Déjà Do—they come in for wigs—so it's not hard not to stare. I pick up the little silk hat and put it back on her head.

We stand together until the T-Bird stops running and Larry and Cornell stumble past us to the tent. Their coveralls are black with muck, and they smell more like wild animals than people.

We really should throw a party under the trees, since they just saved another one, but they look too worn out for that.

"Good night, my crickets," Larry says as he reaches with oil-stained hands for his sponge pillow.

"Night," Cornell whispers, his own blackened hands trembling as he closes his eyes and covers himself with a sheet.

They usually snore and mumble and fart. They usually kick their sheets off and visit the thunderbox at least once. I've known them to turn the radio on and listen until the weatherman gave his forecast, and I've known them to check the time by flashing their watches with their flashlights. But tonight is the hardest I've ever seen them sleep. It's like they dropped their bodies on the ground and their souls went somewhere else.

"Why don't you stay in the house with me, take the spare bedroom?" Mrs. McBean says.

"No, ma'am. My place is outside with them. I'm a Ford man, remember?"

I lie on my pallet and try to make my brain take me back to the dream I was having earlier, but I can never quite get there. Why do dreams have to work that way? Why can't we just pick them up where we left off?

I've barely asked myself these questions when Maggie appears again. This time she's squatting at the door to the tent, looking in with the bill of a Grizzlies cap shading her face. Behind her the sun is up in the trees. The fan's blowing, but it's still so hot you can feel the heat pressing against the walls of the tent.

Maggie's T-shirt says *Get Used to It* in big red letters.

"Get used to what?" I say.

"If you have to ask, then you still have a lot of soul-searching to do," she says. "Besides, I know what you did."

And this is how I understand that I'm not dreaming after all. "You do?" I'm thinking she visited her old house and saw how I cleaned up.

"You and Mrs. McBean danced in the moonlight without me," she says. "Not fair, Jack. Not fair at all."

I sit up and crawl through the door. It's always hard to wake up, but the bright, screaming sunlight this morning really is a pain.

"As nice as I've been to you," she says, "and you couldn't walk over and let me know you got the T-Bird started?"

I begin to mutter an apology, but she cuts me off. "Just kidding!" And she throws her arms around me. "You did it, Jack! You got it started!"

"I didn't . . . I mean, I helped a little but it was . . ."

I point to the tent and make the quiet sign, and Maggie pokes her head in. Larry and Cornell are lying on their backs, arms rigid by their sides. Their bodies are so still you have to watch closely to tell they're breathing.

She summons me with a finger, and I follow her to the porch, where Mrs. McBean is just now stepping out with another one of her trays. "Coffee, anyone?"

"I'll have some," Maggie says.

"You drink coffee, Maggie? Since when? Mrs. McBean didn't know that."

"Granny lets me. I'm not a child anymore, Mrs. McBean." She's smiling at me when she says this.

"If drinking coffee makes you stop being a child," I say, "then I'll always be one. I hate coffee—hate how it tastes, hate how it smells."

"Cream and sugar, lots and lots of sugar," Mrs. McBean says, pouring Maggie a cup. "Let's give you three spoonfuls. Oh, the good things life is made of whether Junior thinks so or not."

There are still some soft drinks in the washtub. The ice

has melted, and they're standing in warm water. I grab one, pop the top, and drain it.

"Worn out, aren't you, Junior?" Mrs. McBean says, and sits forward in her chair. "It's all the hard work, and it's all the striving—yes, that's right, baby, the *striving*! You're not watching TV and playing video games all day. You're not levitating two feet off the ground in your daddy's La-Z-Boy. You're out engaging life with a friendly face and some bullnose pliers, and that isn't easy, is it?"

I shake my head.

"It takes backbone to be a Ford man, doesn't it, Junior?"

I'm not sure she really wants an answer, so I just look at her with the friendly face she mentioned.

"You want another can of pop?" she says. "Go on. Have all you want. Mrs. McBean won't tell your cousins anything."

Across the yard Larry and Cornell spill out of the tent. By now I've accepted that they do nothing the way others do it. Neither of them feels the need to stretch or yawn or even scratch himself. Instead they march over to the T-Bird and start working again.

"What page are you on in your horse book?" Mrs. McBean says. "I ask because I have something in the house I'd like to give you."

"I quit on it. Couldn't take it anymore. The writer kills the pony, then some buzzards come and a big one eats his eye."

"The pony's eye or the writer's?" Maggie says.

"The pony's. What kind of dumb writer does that?"

"Did the pony have a nasty disposition?" Mrs. McBean says.

"No, ma'am. It was a sweet little colt."

"I hear you," Mrs. McBean says. "Junior, go get me that book. I would like to see it."

I've been keeping it in my bag, wrapped up in some underwear that I had a hard time getting clean. I pull it out and accidentally drop it as I'm leaving the tent, then I accidentally kick it. By the time I reach the back porch I've accidentally torn the cover.

"Steinbeck," Mrs. McBean says when I hand her the book. "And he killed the pony, did he?"

"Yes, ma'am."

She hands the book to Maggie. "Maggie, go throw it over the fence into Mr. Reuben's yard. See if you can't reach his bushes. I could tolerate a little horse dying, but not the buzzard-eating-the-eye part. That is sick."

Maggie has a better arm than mine. She throws it high and far, and I can hear it smack against the empty slab where Mr. Reuben would've had his home. She returns to the porch and falls back in a chair, her chest heaving.

"Excellent job," Mrs. McBean says. "No buzzards pecking out a pony's eyes in *The Magical Land of Noom*. None in *Hitty*, either. No, sir. Preston dreamed about being a writer—a *book* writer, I should say, since he already wrote for the paper. But I couldn't see him doing that even to a big grown horse that kicked somebody. Listen, Junior, you are welcome to Preston's books. Take any you want. But there is one in particular I would like for you to have."

"No, ma'am. I couldn't do that to you."

"Do it to me? What are you talking about? It's *Adventures of Huckleberry Finn*. Don't you want his copy?"

"No, ma'am. It's yours."

"And Mrs. McBean is giving it to you—a first edition. Take it on the road with you. Read it and write me a book report."

She gets up and disappears in the house, and Maggie says, "I don't understand the old-people generation, thinking that one's any good. You'll see." She sips her coffee, but it's a small sip—more a test than an actual sip. When the cup leaves her mouth, I can see a baby lipstick print on the rim.

"You're going to have dragon breath, drinking that stuff."

She takes another sip, one that goes on for a good minute. Then she breathes on me, right in my face. "So disrespectful," she says. "Sometimes I don't know why I even talk to you."

The book is old and raggedy. The cover's a hard, green board with gold lettering that's mostly rubbed off. It shows Huck wearing a straw hat. He looks a little like a kid at my school—a kid I can't stand.

"Preston found it at a garage sale," Mrs. McBean says. "I can see him sitting in his chair and flipping through it, looking for where they mentioned Cairo."

I open to the first page and see *10¢* written in pencil in the corner.

"Yours now," she says.

"But I can't."

"No, Junior. You *can*. And you will. Mrs. McBean believes books are meant to be read, not to sit on a shelf. If you finish it and don't think it's any good, throw it over a fence. But if it has artistic merit and you get something from it, pass it on to the next reader. Or, even better, donate it to your local public library. Y'all have a library in Sheboygan Falls, don't you, Junior?"

"It looks like a bunker. That's what Daddy says."

"It's not how it looks on the outside that counts. It's the inside that's important, where they keep the dreams. Oh, did I just say dreams? Mrs. McBean meant books, not that there's any difference."

Across the yard Cornell is digging around in the Time Sensitive cooler and loading the camp table with things to cook. There's bacon, eggs, and a tube of those biscuits that come already buttered with fake butter.

He uses the Dutch oven for the biscuits, but the rest goes straight into his skillet. It's always exciting to watch him cook— "Like a Broadway show," Mrs. McBean says—and the smell is unreal.

Unable to take it any longer, Larry hobbles over and steals a strip of half-cooked bacon. Cornell squawks and takes a swipe at him with his plastic flipper.

Larry's still chewing when he walks over to the porch.

"May I have a word with you, Mrs. McBean?" he says. It takes a moment for him to swallow.

"You can have as many words as you like. You know that."

"Well, it's running pretty good, but that's not the same as being road ready. I regret to report that cousin Cornell put his foot through your floor pan last night. The pan supports the floorboards down where you put your feet and operate your gas and brake pedals. We'll need to rebuild it before anybody can expect to get behind the wheel. We can do the job with fiberglass and resin, but the more expedient option is to cut plywood to fit the hole. I've got a half-inch sheet in the truck."

"Do that. Do the wood."

"Yes, ma'am."

"And put that on Mrs. McBean's tab, will you?"

He doesn't respond to this last part. "Your brakes are another problem. Again, it's rust. There's so much we can't even turn the wheels. Your exhaust system also needs work—more than work. We need to change it."

"The T-bird's sick, isn't it? Sick as Mrs. McBean."

"I'm sorry." And his shoulders slump. "It's just proving to be a bigger job than we anticipated. We are basically doing patchwork, but you still should be prepared. Even if you are paying for parts only, it's going to be expensive."

"What's another bill if I get to peel out again?"

"Yes, madam." Larry pivots and looks at me now. "Hungry, June? We're going to need you today. Lots to do, son."

I never popped the top on that second soda, so I put the can back in the water. "Ready," I say.

"And you, young lady?" He's talking to the coffee drinker. "Come get a bite to eat. We could use another pair of hands."

Maggie hops off the porch and takes off running to where Cornell is loading the plates. "I'm a Ford man!" she yells. "A Ford man! I'm a Ford man!"

I could describe it all in great detail, but I doubt you really want to hear it. Basically, it's a long afternoon of plugging holes and changing parts. The thing I like best is bossing Maggie around. The thing I like least is when she bosses me around, which turns out to be most of the day. She knows the names of tools better than I do, and she's even handled a reciprocating saw before. After Cornell sizes up the plywood, he lets Maggie cut it with the saw, and wouldn't you know it's a perfect fit for the floor pan.

"You amaze me," I tell her in a quiet voice.

"How about me, huh? I really do need to give the credit to Granny. She taught me everything I know."

"And how is that?"

"Only the two of us. No money to hire a Mr. Fix-It. How else?"

Cornell must see that my confidence is shaken, so he lets me use some kind of power tool to drive in the rivets connecting the wood to the steel frame. I think those are rivets I'm driving. Cornell's sucking on sunflower seeds when he shows me how to do it, and this makes him difficult to understand, so if it isn't rivets it's divots, even though I've always thought divots were the holes a golf club makes when you're swinging at the ball and bang the ground instead, kicking up a clod.

Next we work on the exhaust, and our job—Maggie's and mine—is to dispose of the old pieces and to hand them the replacements. They must tell us a hundred times that we're like the nurse in the operating room when the surgeon says, "Scalpel," and sticks out a hand for one. I know they're trying to make us feel like we're making an important contribution. And it must work, because Maggie keeps saying, "Yes, Doctor," and reaching over with a shop cloth to clean the sweat from my cousins' faces.

It's a little embarrassing when I have to visit the thunderbox, but the way I look at it, that's what Larry and Cornell get for pushing so much breakfast on me. You don't eat eggs and bacon and seven biscuits with fake butter without upsetting the pipes. Maybe next time when I say a protein bar's enough, they will listen.

When I finish and step back outside, there's lime dusting my shoes. And Maggie is nowhere to be found, not that I'm upset about that. It's a relief that I don't have to account for being gone so long.

"Where'd she go?" I ask Larry and Cornell.

They're busy banging the rust off the brake drums, so their response is what you'd expect: "Who . . . *huh* . . . what?"

"Maggie. What happened to her?"

"Oh, she had to go home," Larry says. He laughs a little. "She asked us to tell you she hoped everything came out okay."

Mrs. McBean is in her kitchen and once again thumbing through bills. The look on her face is one I know well. It's the same look Mama always has at the end of the month.

"I wish I was rich," she says. "Not for me but for everyone who needs their money."

When it's not on the back porch, she keeps the pumpkin head with the Halloween candy on the counter next to the stove. She gets up now and holds the thing at just the right angle. I can see everything inside.

"Sometimes I can hear the candy calling," she says. "The M&M's and the Baby Ruths. 'Eat me, eat me,' they're saying. Nobody likes being unloved, not even the Blow Pops and Jolly Ranchers. Does Mrs. McBean sound like she needs to go on *Dr. Phil*? Please, Junior, have yourself some Hot Tamales. I won't tell anyone if you don't tell anyone."

You don't want to disappoint the person who just gave you her husband's copy of *Huckleberry Finn*. So I spend the next hour in the kitchen eating my way through her stash and listening to her talk. I smile every fifteen seconds or so to let her know I'm not missing anything.

It's true that I'm playing hooky from my job handing out scalpels in the operating room, but I can tell she needs me more than Larry and Cornell do. When I look out to check on how they're doing, they are both in total android mode. There's no point in pretending I'd do anything but get in the way.

"I quit on my treatments," Mrs. McBean says. "The chemo was making me feel worse than the cancer did, and I had enough and said *no más*."

Because the hospital in Cairo shut down years ago, Maggie's grandmother drove her to a cancer center in Paducah, Kentucky, for appointments—an hour there, an hour back. It's one thing to impose upon your neighbor for a cup of sugar, but quite another to ask her to take you on a long road trip every few weeks.

"To be honest," she says. "I didn't mind losing my hair. One less job to do in the morning."

She does what she can where the bills are concerned. She always sends something, even if it's short of what they ask for, because she can only stretch her social security checks so far. She's pleasant to the bill collectors, including those who threaten to ruin her. "But Mrs. McBean is already ruined, baby" is her favorite comeback.

She believes in heaven. It won't be long before she's with Preston again, and they will be in their young, healthy bodies, and they'll be given another chance at life. She won't let him work on any dangerous stories next time, and they won't wait on having children. Lately a little girl's been coming to her in her dreams. Pretty little thing asking Mrs. McBean to braid her hair or to pour her a bowl of cereal and milk. Walking around the house dragging a chubby doll by the arm. Mama this and Mama that. Can I sleep with you and Papa tonight?

And who is Papa? Does she really have to tell me?

The dreams are so real she can't believe it when she wakes up and finds the house empty but for Moose in the bed with her.

Outside, Larry and Cornell have cranked the T-Bird again, and the sound it makes is more like a throaty rumble than a squealing clatter. The car's still loud, but it's a different kind of loud, deep and contented rather than shrill and plaintive.

The phone rings, competing with the car for our attention. When Mrs. McBean covers her face with her hands and starts shaking her head, I get up and punch the talk button, prepared to let them have it, but a familiar voice says, "Mrs. McBean? *Hello?* Mrs. McBean, I'm trying to find Maggie. She's not still over there with you, is she?"

TWENTY

I HURRY OVER AND CHECK the storage room where they keep the bikes. "The Raleigh's gone," I say.

Her grandmother's standing at the door, a look on her face like Mama's when she believes things can't get any worse.

"Can I borrow your Schwinn? It shouldn't take long."

"Go, *go*," she says, hurrying me off with a wave.

I ride as fast as I can. Once I turn the corner and start getting close, I can see Maggie's bike lying in the grass, same place as before. I drop the Schwinn next to it without braking. I land on my feet at a run, my momentum carrying me forward. The pile of trash bags is still on the side of the house. I open the front door and step inside, and everything looks right. By that I mean there aren't any squatters waiting to murder me for discovering that they murdered Maggie.

Upstairs all the doors are open but hers. I give it three soft knocks. "Maggie? Maggie, it's Jack."

It's the first time I've ever actually called myself that

except in my head. When she doesn't answer—when nobody does—I say, "It's me, Maggie. Please. Are you in there?"

Am I scared? Scared of who'll open it? Scared of what I'll find? Better believe I am. But the door swings open, and next thing you know she's hugging me.

"Jack," she says, and I feel her face all wet against the side of mine.

"What's wrong? What are you crying for?"

"Oh, I don't know. Just got to feeling sorry for myself, thinking about everything. I was doing so well, helping you and your cousins, when suddenly I realized what I was doing. I was helping you finish the job so you could leave, when I should've been doing the opposite, breaking more things to make sure you stayed."

The picnic blanket's on the floor over where she said her bed used to be. I also see a flashlight, a gallon jug of water, and a pimento cheese sandwich in a plastic carton.

"I tried to talk to Granny about it," she says. "She was patient with me at first, but then she said, 'Oh, my, are we struggling with abandonment issues again?' She didn't mean to hurt me, but her tone just about did me in. Like we'd already covered that territory and it shouldn't matter anymore."

"I'd never do that," I say.

"Do what?"

"Abandon you. You're my friend, Maggie, maybe the only real one I have."

She moves to the windows and looks outside, away from

me. "You'll start sixth grade," she says. "Then seventh. We'll be in high school and I'll send you a friend request and you'll say, 'Maggie Moore? Now who was that again?'" She turns back to me. "Thank you for what you did. Cleaning the house and all? And don't say it was nothing. It was a *lot*, and it was sweet and wonderful. I will always remember you for that."

If always being remembered is what you get for helping somebody out, then I need to get busy looking for more houses to clean.

"Let's go home, Maggie," I say. "Granny's worried."

"This is home. I won't ever leave again."

I can't tell if she's serious. I think she might be. At the same time, maybe what she really needs is for me to talk her out of it.

"Can you imagine how spooky it must be in this place at night?"

"Spooky? Not to me."

"People were here before, Maggie. They left their trash everywhere. Their clothes. What if they come back?"

"I can defend myself. I took karate. Ask Granny."

"No electricity or running water. I'll tell you something else. Pimento cheese sucks. I know my cheeses, and that stuff is gross. Let's go home."

"This is home."

"Then let's go to your other house. Granny needs to know nothing's wrong. So does Mrs. McBean."

Not that this is any earth-shattering revelation, but girls

are different. Sometimes all they have left is to make a big production.

I take the blanket off the floor and tuck it under my arm. I carry the water and the flashlight, and she carries the sandwich. At the top of the stairs, gazing down at the floor below, Maggie says, "How long did it take?"

"Not long."

"Now you're really making me feel bad. I saw all the bags. It's like an army was here, and it was only you. Hours, I bet. Hours and hours."

On the ride back to her grandmother's, I wait until she glances back at me, and then I pretend to lose control of the bike. I make it wobble and swing from one side of the street to the other. I add to the con by poking my tongue out and twisting my face in horror. It gets the laugh I'm after—a big one, a Maggie laugh.

"Woo-woo-woo," she says into the wind.

"Woo-woo-woo," I answer.

This might be a little off since I'm the guy who's saying it, but there's a responsibility that comes with loving somebody. What I didn't understand until this summer is that there's also one that comes with being loved.

You can't just cut and run when you stop believing you're any good. There's a kid waiting in an empty house for the chance to show you how wrong you are. There's another one on the road looking for you in every town, in every store and car, in rest areas and river parks, day and night.

Are you hearing me, Mr. and Mrs. Moore?

What about you, Daddy?

They run their tests on the neighborhood streets. Larry drives and Cornell rides shotgun, then they reverse roles and Cornell drives and Larry rides shotgun. They work the car up to forty miles per hour going in one direction, then they slow it down, U-turn, and see how fast they can make it go in the other direction.

On four or five occasions they pull into deserted lots and mess around with the engine, talking in the mysterious language of cars that non–car people don't understand. On the straightaways they gun the T-Bird hard and brake hard.

The more they drive the better the engine sounds, and the less smoke comes shooting from the car's backside.

Mrs. McBean watches from the shade of her front porch, Moose in her arms barking like crazy. I whistle every time the T-Bird races past, and Maggie one-ups me by whistling even louder.

It's good to see her rebound so quickly.

Before now I'd wondered what Mrs. McBean's reaction would be when she saw the T-Bird running the roads again, and I'll be honest, it's different from what I imagined. There's no big celebration, and she doesn't let on that she's seeing her past brought roaring back from the dead.

"Me next," I hear her say once, but that's it.

As the car moves farther and farther away, the engine

sounds like distant thunder, and all that's left to see are occasional flashes of light over the tall weeds of the abandoned lawns. The flashes are the sun striking glass or metal. They look like sparks from a welder's torch.

Cornell stops the car in the middle of the street and waves me over. Then he remembers Maggie and gestures for her to join us. We get in close to him like football players in a huddle waiting for the quarterback to call the next play. "You two squeeze in together on the passenger side," he says. "It wouldn't be running without your help, so what say we go for a ride?"

It really was an honor to work on the T-Bird, but I never wanted to ride in it. I still don't. Something happened the last time Mr. McBean rode in it, and the thought of it haunts me enough. "I'm going to stay here," I say, "if that's okay with you, cousin."

"Me, too," Maggie says. "Thanks, though."

Cornell stands tall and looks over at Mrs. McBean. She's still over on the porch and still watching.

"Yeah, sure," he says, the wind blowing his whiskers like a flag.

Once all the tests are done, Cornell wheels the car off the street and follows Larry to the backyard. They park it under the trees. "First on race day," they shout at exactly the same time.

"*F-o-r-d*," I say to myself, breaking the words down by their first letters.

Cornell strokes the dashboard the way I stroke Moose when she needs it, and then he kills the engine.

The sudden silence brings its own noise, a kind of rolling ocean roar. I wait until my hearing has adjusted. "Will we stick around to see Mrs. McBean peel out?" I say.

"That depends on Mrs. McBean," Larry says. "But I can tell you our clients are tired of my calls and texts about unforeseen delays and schedule changes. We should be going."

"How can we leave now?" I argue. "It would be like walking out on a movie right before the end."

"Well, that might be so, June. But tell that to Mr. Palermo in Alamogordo who called five times yesterday saying he couldn't wait any longer." He shakes his head as if tormented by the recollection of the calls.

"He can't wait another half day? What's twelve hours? So what if we get there at six P.M. instead of six A.M."

Larry waits for me to look at him. "Is this about the T-Bird or something else?" When I don't answer, it only makes him stare harder. "I know you and Maggie have become friends, June, and I'm sorry you have to say goodbye. But it goes with being a Ford man. You know that."

I swallow and can feel my Adam's apple slide up and down my neck.

"There was a '52 Ranch Wagon up Klamath Falls way," he says now in a different voice, this one calmer and more patient. "We could hear the owner every morning singing through an open window when she had her bath. It was prettier than any songbird, June, way prettier, and I suppose I've never fully recovered. Sometimes in the quiet, when there is quiet, I can still hear her voice and the song she liked to sing. Do you know 'Moon River' by chance?"

I shake my head.

He takes his phone out of his pocket and swipes the face until he finds what he's looking for. I thought it was going to be a recording of 'Moon River,' but instead it's Mrs. McBean from a month ago, begging us to hurry. There's a pause, a long one, then she says, "*Please!*" and hangs up.

How many times have I heard people say that word? How many times have I said it? "*Please!*" Mrs. McBean says, as if her life depended on it.

"Okay," Larry says. "We'll stay a little longer. But only a little."

TWENTY-ONE

THERE'S A MAN SITTING with Mrs. McBean on the back porch. The screen makes it hard to see. He's holding Moose with one hand and picking at the candy in the pumpkin head with the other. Does it bother me that he's intruded on my territory? Yes, it does. He and Mrs. McBean have been speaking in hushed tones. I can't tell what they're saying.

"Who's that man over there?" I say.

Larry and Cornell have been making paella in a huge pan, and the smell is so incredible I swear I could take a bite out of my arm.

"Mr. Faircloth," Cornell says.

I don't know why my brain doesn't serve up the man's image right away, but I do see headlights on a metal building and a sign over a giant door.

"Oh, right. The collector guy. The dude in pajamas."

"Mr. Faircloth is many things, June," Cornell says, "but

I'm not sure a dude in pajamas is one of them." He shoots me a look that tells me to be nice.

"What's he doing here?" I ask.

Cornell lifts the pan from the cookstove and starts flipping the rice.

"He came to speak to Mrs. McBean," Larry answers, in a casual sort of way.

I'm confused. Mr. Faircloth knows Mrs. McBean? How is that?

I guess she gets tired of me staring at them from across the lawn. She stands and nudges the screen door open. "Junior, come over here, boy. That's right. Mrs. McBean wants you to meet somebody."

Mr. Faircloth is holding his hand out when I get there. I shake it, and my first thought is, *How was he able to get a mitt that big in my pumpkin head?*

Instead of a robe and pajamas he's wearing a rumpled T-shirt and dirty khakis that barely reach his ankles. Whiskers stand out on his face, and a little dried booger hugs the rim of his right nostril. He's normal-looking, normal in every way. By that I mean he doesn't look like somebody with a lot of money, not that I've ever met one of those people before.

"At long last," he says. "Wow, what a pleasure. It's June Ball. Your cousins and Mrs. McBean have told me a lot about you."

"Don't worry, it's all good," Mrs. McBean says. "Junior, sit with us, baby, and take Moose, will you? Mr. Faircloth's had enough."

"Not at all," he says, giving me a wink as he hands her over.

"Mr. Faircloth wants to buy the T-Bird, Junior. He likes the provenance. I wasn't sure what a provenance was until Mr. Faircloth explained it." She pauses and lets out a sigh. "Preston," she says. "Preston is the provenance."

"Whose story is a part of a tragic but important chapter of American history," adds Mr. Faircloth.

"Oh, come on now, Mr. Faircloth. I can appreciate that, I really can, but Preston was never the story—he was just working the story. I don't know why a reporter had to die. If it was to inspire people who see his car to learn about Cairo and what happened to Private Hunt . . . well, I'm sorry but that still is not enough." She pivots slightly in her chair and faces me. "Junior, Mr. Faircloth is making plans to open a museum for his Ford collection. He thinks the T-Bird belongs in it. What do you think about that?"

"I don't know anything about museums," I say, "but I do think people need to see it. It's more than just a car, Mrs. McBean."

"Fifty thousand dollars," she announces suddenly, not seeming impressed by the figure. "Mr. Faircloth says that you and your cousins will have to reinstall the old windshield. And why is that again, Mr. Faircloth? Tell Junior."

"The hole tells the story."

"Ah, right. The hole tells the story. Well, what do you say, Junior? Does Mrs. McBean accept the offer?"

Maybe if I hadn't seen his airstrip and airplane and pilot and rows of metal buildings already crowded with rows of antique cars. Maybe if there weren't so many bills on Mrs. McBean's kitchen table. And maybe if her phone would just stop ringing for a minute, I wouldn't say what I say now: "Can you do better, Mr. Faircloth? I hate to insult you, sir, but your offer's too low for a car that belongs in a museum. I heard Larry and Cornell talking the other day about a Mustang that sold for over a million dollars at auction."

"Yes," he says, "and I'm the one who bought it. But that was a Shelby, June, and a prototype. In other words, it was by a famous designer, Carroll Shelby, and it was the first one he ever made. This is a different deal altogether."

I look down at Moose, and she reaches up and licks me. "Better. I still say you can do better."

He shifts in his chair and faces Mrs. McBean, and his tongue makes a slow turn around his lips. "All things considered, ma'am, a hundred thousand dollars is as high as I can go. I'm sorry I can't pay more, but that's my final offer."

It's like we're not there all of a sudden. Mr. Faircloth isn't there, and neither am I.

She's staring across the lawn at the T-Bird. "Will she get to drive it first?"

"I beg your pardon?" Mr. Faircloth says.

"Mrs. McBean," Mrs. McBean answers. "Will she get to drive the car first?"

"Oh, yes, ma'am. Drive it all you like."

"I wish I could call Preston and ask him. He would know what to do." She lets out another sigh. "It's a lot of money, Mr. Faircloth, and it would go a long way with the bills. Thank you for your offer. Mind if I sleep on it tonight?"

"Take your time, ma'am."

"Time," she says with a chuckle. "Boy, do I like the sound of that."

I miss the actual moment when Mr. Faircloth leaves.

He and Mrs. McBean spend another hour on the porch, and then she limps over to the tent and slumps in the Campeche chair, her back to the T-Bird, Moose asleep in the pocket of her housedress.

She's holding a glass even though there's nothing in it, and she's chewing on a pink Starburst from her Halloween hoard. "I offered him the guest bedroom," she says. "He told me he already had accommodations. 'In *Cairo*?' I said. 'Where is that?'" She uncorks a big laugh now, unable to help it. "He said at a private airfield just north of here. He's going to sleep on his plane."

She wheels around for a look over her shoulder, as if to confront someone who just whispered in her ear. But it's the T-Bird she is facing.

"Please forgive me, darling," I think she says, the words a mumble.

Cornell takes her glass and puts it in the pan for dirty

dishes. He and Larry are still double-teaming the paella. "Would you like a drink, ma'am?"

"Well . . ." She leans forward with her elbows on her thighs. "What about grappa? You don't have any, do you?"

"Coming right up," Cornell says, and steps over to the truck. You can hear him banging around in back, then he re-appears with a bottle topped with a cork.

"Enjoy," he says when he finishes filling a cup.

I have a look at it. "What is grappa?"

"Grappa? Oh, that's an adult beverage made from grapes. Helps with your digestion." She drains the cup and pours herself another one. "Mrs. McBean hopes it also helps with a guilty mind. She could use that."

"Are you guilty about selling the T-Bird?"

"Yes, I am, Junior. For years Mrs. McBean stayed mad at the car, growling every time she sat on the porch and looked over that way. There were days when Mrs. McBean hated it. Why else would I let the thing continue to fall apart like that? Now Mrs. McBean understands it's a victim like Preston was. The T-Bird had a life ahead of it. Roads to travel. They were stolen, too."

Over at the cookstove Larry is adding pepper flakes, while Cornell adds lemon zest. Then one is adjusting the flame, while the other's spooning up taste tests. The wonder is that they never bump into each other. I'd almost rather watch them than the Packers.

Maggie and her grandmother show up after a while. I don't know if they were invited or if they got a whiff of the paella and came running over. Our semicircle is one chair short, so Larry gets a spare from the truck. Next he finds the radio and turns it on.

So far this summer we've listened to a lot of classical, country, and bluegrass, with occasional breaks for R & B and blues. There's been rock, hip-hop, bebop, pop, funk, and swing. But the station he lands on now is the first to play disco. "Thank you, Alexa," Cornell says, and frames the words on his apron with matching oven mitts. "Thank you for blessing us with 'Funkytown' tonight."

In the song a car horn sounds, and now both Larry and Cornell add their own horns: *Bee beep!* A lady is singing, and they sing along with her, getting every word right. Cornell lowers the flames under the paella, and he and Larry start dancing around the cookstove like robots: mechanical arms and legs pumping, square heads bobbing to the beat.

I'm embarrassed for them. You never want to laugh at people—better to laugh *with* them, Mama says—but I have to do it. They asked for it.

Maggie starts laughing, too. That is, until she jumps out of her chair and starts dancing with them.

I wish I could tell you it ends with just the three of them being fools, but then Mrs. McBean is on her feet, becoming the fourth fool. The best she can do is rock Moose in her arms a little, but she's into it, you can tell.

I give her a thumbs-up, and she gives me one back.

Granny's been moving to the music, and she can't seem to take sitting in her chair another minute. She's up next.

Five fools now. Six if you count Moose.

I suppose it was inevitable: Now they're all looking at me.

"No way. Nah-uhn. Forget about it."

Did you really think that would stop them? Maggie comes over with her arms out, her fingers playing invisible synthesizer keys. "Trust me," she says.

"I can't."

"Trust me, Jack."

And so I do. I get up out of my chair. And I trust her.

TWENTY-TWO

"OF COURSE WE CAN NEVER say a word about this for the rest of our lives," Maggie says when the song ends.

Her grandmother hides her face in her hands. "Mrs. McBean, I thought you said it was grape juice."

Larry and Cornell serve the paella on real china. By that I mean no paper or plastic. I keep taking trips to the cookstove, one after another. I probably should just ditch my plate, grab a spoon, and eat straight from the pan.

"Does Preston's radio work?" Mrs. McBean asks. "The one in the T-Bird, I should say."

"It does," Larry says. "But it's AM only. Might be hard to get good reception."

"What about the headlights?"

"Yes, madam. The headlights work fine."

"And the taillights?"

"They're good, Mrs. McBean. Everything works."

"Mr. Faircloth wants to display the car just the way it is," she says. "I argued for a complete restoration. Make it how it was. Let people know what a sweet dream the car was once. He wouldn't hear of it."

"Yes," Larry says. "To most the T-Bird's just an old rust bucket, but to the history student there's beauty in its appearance. Ravaged by life's storms, it's still with us, still fighting, unwilling to give up."

Everyone stops eating as his words hang in the air. It's Maggie who finally says, "Are you sure you're describing the T-Bird, Mr. Larry?"

We all turn to Mrs. McBean. She gives a smile to let us know she's been asking herself the same question. "Call Mr. Faircloth and tell him it's a deal," she says. "He can make the check out to Lila McBean. Have him deduct what I owe you."

"Yes, madam."

"Thank you for a lovely evening. Mrs. McBean is leaving Funkytown now and going to bed."

We watch her navigate the lawn to the porch, her steps so shaky it's a wonder she doesn't topple over. Even the T-Bird seems to be watching her. As soon as she enters the house, Larry removes the phone from his pocket.

He walks over to the thunderbox and makes the call. "Hello . . . Hello, Mr. Faircloth." We can barely hear him, but more random words follow: "First thing . . . Car hauler . . . Hospice . . . I know, I know . . . Devastating . . . Yes yes *yes* . . . Congratulations . . . Good night, sir . . ."

"Will you escort us home, please?" Granny says.

A moment passes before I realize she's talking to me. "Yes, ma'am."

They thank Larry and Cornell with air-kisses, and we walk around the side of the house. By the time we reach the street Granny has added several yards to the distance between herself and Maggie and me. I suspect she's giving us some privacy.

"I hate this part," Maggie says. "But I don't have to tell you that, do I, Jack?"

"What's amazing is that it happens to Larry and Cornell all the time. I don't know how they stand it."

"Granny says they're some kind of supernatural beings, not angels exactly, but close. Spirit animals."

"Does she also think that about me?"

"No, Jack. We can tell you're a regular boy."

Up ahead, porch and carport lights are shining at Maggie's house. Her grandmother moves toward the front door, a shadow stretching behind her as she gets closer. She uses a key to let herself in, then we hear an electronic belch when she turns off the house alarm. I glance at the sky, the moon shining over Cairo.

"Did they say when you're heading out exactly?"

"No, but it'll be tonight or early in the morning."

She crosses her arms over her chest. It's as if she needs to protect herself from what she's about to say. "Some of the old days around here might've sucked, but that doesn't mean our new ones have to. I'm going to college. I want to be a doctor and help people. I love Cairo, and I'm coming back when I finish med school. First I'll open an office, then a clinic that offers more than just routine care, then a hospital—a big one. Cancer patients like Mrs. McBean shouldn't have such a hard time getting the treatments they need. I know the odds are against me, but I'm not myself unless I'm dreaming. What do you want to be, Jack? A mechanic?"

I look at her a long time. "Couldn't tell you," I say. "But, no, not a mechanic. I like Fords and all, but I never had a call to fix them."

"Mrs. McBean taught Granny in second grade. Did you know that?"

I shake my head.

"The regular teacher was out on a maternity leave—out for months—and the school brought Mrs. McBean in to take her place. Granny says it was Mrs. McBean who taught her how to read. Imagine how cool it must be to be a teacher explaining to children what those little marks on the page mean."

"I really like hair," I tell her, finally saying it. "Guess I'm like my mom that way. Maybe I could have my own place."

"What kind? Like a barbershop?"

I don't know why I can't say it, but the words get stuck and won't come out. I can see her grandmother's silhouette in one of the windows, and I can see the moon coming even closer. Plenty of men own salons, and plenty of them cut women's hair. I don't see why it's such a big deal.

"I can't wait until I'm old," Maggie says. "What about you?"

"I don't know. Maybe. I need to find my dad first."

She nods and offers her hand, and as we're shaking out there in the street a crazy thing happens. She moves closer at the same time I do, and our faces come together, our lips too. So what if I have to get up on my tiptoes? It's another first for me, and another gift from the road. "Good meeting you, Jack."

"Yeah. You, too, Maggie."

I really shouldn't run back to Mrs. McBean's. It might make Maggie think I didn't like what just happened. But I'm excited and my legs have something else in mind.

"Walk," I tell them. "Come on, boys." My mouth won't listen, either. "Please don't," I tell it. The next instant it yells, "Maggie Moore!"

"Jack Ball!" Maggie answers as I turn my arms and legs into pistons.

I don't think I've ever moved so fast.

The truck's loaded and ready to go, but they decide to wait until morning. "Bloody grapes," Larry says, looking as if he really does blame them.

Since the tent's packed away, they lie in the grass and resume their cadaver poses. I stretch out between them and remember back to how everybody looked dancing under the trees. When exactly do I fall asleep? It is hard to know. Maybe as I was starting to pray for Cairo. I don't think I dream, but next thing I know a loud rumble is making the ground shake.

I jump to my feet, and so do Larry and Cornell. Somebody must've just shot off a rocket.

But, no, it's the T-Bird again. The top is down and so are the windows. As Mrs. McBean reverses past us I can see her face in the light from the dash. It might sound hokey, but there's a peace about her that I never saw before. I can also see Moose perched on the passenger seat. She's trembling, terrified of what's to come.

"Where will you be taking her, madam?" Larry says.

"The Point, I think. Yes, where the rivers meet."

Cornell moves to the middle of the yard and helps Mrs. McBean navigate the narrow space next to the truck. Then we follow her to the driveway and out to the street.

The sun is coming up over Cairo now, and golden light spins in the warm, dusty air. It really is a fine morning for a drive.

"Be safe, madam."

"I will, thank you."

"Will you be gone long?"

Mrs. McBean shrugs. "I don't know. I suppose it depends on what I find when I get there."

"We have to be on the road again, madam. Another Ford, I'm afraid."

She nods to show she understands, then she has a last look at each of us. For the smallest moment, when she settles on me, she no longer looks old and sick. Some miracle has happened and she's young again. The world is better than it was, and people get along. Nothing has happened yet, and nothing ever will.

"I love you," she says. "Mr. Larry. Mr. Cornell. *Junior!* Yes, you, Junior. Mrs. McBean loves her sweet boy."

We begin to answer, but she cranks the radio and a love song comes on, one from long ago. I think I've heard it before but can't remember when or where.

"What is that one?" I begin to say. But Mrs. McBean hits the gas and accelerates, the wheels squealing as they dig for traction.

Mama always had a fit when Daddy drove too fast. She didn't understand why he was in such a hurry in his pickup when it was so hard to get him out of his chair on the porch. But I did, I understood.

It's something Larry said one night on the road: "Human beings are never more alive, June, than when they're going somewhere fast."

After Mrs. McBean and Moose and the T-Bird are gone, all that's left are planks of steaming rubber on the pavement.

TWENTY-THREE

WE DO A '49 CUSTOM in Pipestone, Minnesota, then head to Davenport, Iowa, for a '69 Capri. Both are three-day jobs with day trips between them.

Wherever we are now, I'm sleeping when we stop. The doors open and close at the exact same time, and I slide down and lay my head on the seat. I can hear their steps outside, and because I've been with them so long, I can tell which pair belong to Larry and which to Cornell.

Next comes the sound of something sliding on a track, and I suddenly feel light on my face.

"Welcome, friends," says a voice that's instantly identifiable.

And that's what does it. That's what gets me up.

We're at Faircloth Motors, and I can't tell if it's late at night or early in the morning. The door to the building is open, and a Ford is parked in the middle of the floor. It's a 1955 Thunderbird convertible, and a team of men and women in matching uniforms is working on it. The engine has been removed and hangs by chains from the rafters, and the body is undergoing restoration. I squint against the lights bouncing off the primer coat.

"What changed your mind?" Larry asks. He is staring at the car, but his question is addressed to Mr. Faircloth.

"Mrs. McBean," he says. "She told me she wanted it how it was, but I wouldn't listen, failing to consider what that hole in the windshield represented to her. I might've seen it as a powerful symbol of the civil rights movement, but to Mrs. McBean it meant only loss. I flew out feeling so righteous I couldn't stand myself, but my conscience wouldn't let it go. Who was I to exploit her husband's passing? Did his last moment really matter more than all his other moments? I felt like I needed to see her again and talk some more, so I had Jimmy turn around and take me back. I pulled up at Mrs. McBean's house, and she and Moose were waiting on the front porch. She walked out and gave me a hug and held my face in her hands. She said she knew I'd be back."

Mr. Faircloth is in his pajamas and bathrobe. He's holding his Ford coffee cup. Off in the distance I can see his plane at the end of the lighted strip.

"What's that one?" Cornell says. He shoots a thumb at an old tank parked outside. It sits in a narrow band of darkness just past the door. There isn't a blue oval on the grill, but the letters along the front of the hood say *Ford*.

"Showed up yesterday on a flatbed," Mr. Faircloth says.

"It's a '66 LTD, not that uncommon, but wait until you hear the backstory."

Larry and Cornell follow him to where the car is parked. I turn on the truck's headlights, then hit them with the brights, and only now do they seem to remember that I've been in the cab the whole time. They motion for me to join them.

"Check this out, June," Cornell says. "You won't believe it. Mr. Faircloth has an astronaut's car."

Mr. Faircloth gets the old bomb started and slides out. He's straightening his robe and pajamas as he walks around to the passenger side. "June, what say we take it for a test run. Come on, my boy. I'll ride shotgun. Let's drive it down to the landing strip and see if it's got anything left."

It's not my first time behind the wheel. That would've been with Daddy in his pickup on Hickory Street, only last year.

Larry and Cornell stand back a safe distance as Mr. Faircloth helps me maneuver the car down to the plane. I think of Mrs. Barnwell doing her scoop wave that time in Piggott, because that's how they're waving to me now. Mr. Faircloth is more than riding shotgun. He's actually sitting right next to me, and he's helping me turn the wheel and operate the pedals. "Big old boat, isn't it, June?" he says. He seems to understand that I'd rather be driving the car alone, because when we get it facing the strip he slides over and gives me more room.

"All yours," Mr. Faircloth says.

It's a straight shot, nothing to it. The lights speed by faster and faster the faster we go until they're only one light. I forget that Mr. Faircloth's with me after a while, and I'd probably still be driving if he doesn't reach over with his foot and hit the brakes. We start skidding all over the place, fishtailing, and I finally think to turn the wheel hard to the left. "Hang on, Mr. Faircloth!" I shout as I feel myself surrendering to the will of the car.

Somehow when we stop spinning we've made a one-eighty and we're facing in the other direction.

The ants down at the end of the strip are Larry and Cornell, and it looks like they're celebrating, jumping up and down, arms over their heads.

"Well done, June," Mr. Faircloth says. "Now take it back to the house."

He's barely finished talking when I punch the gas. Our heads rock back and the lights start coming.

There are more roads and Fords than you can imagine. We add more stars to the Gulf Oil map. One day, if there's time, the whole wrinkled thing will be blue.

Somewhere out on the road I crack open *Huckleberry Finn* and start reading. I go at it for nearly two hours. Cornell's driving, and he must see that I'm not getting very far. "Any good?" he says.

"No, sir. It's terrible."

"It's terrible?"

"They keep saying a bad word. Every time I get to it I feel like I'm doing something wrong."

"What's it about?"

"Huck. Dumb things happen. The river back in his day is like the road today, I understand that much."

"I tried reading it once, long time ago," Cornell says. "I couldn't get past the first chapter—there were no Fords in it. Here's a sorry confession for you, June: I've never read a book in my life. Not a whole one. Everything I am is in my hands. My brain just wasn't built for words."

"If it was built for anything," Larry says. He's been drawing again, but he stops now to let himself laugh. Cornell laughs along with him. They're really going at it, but of course I have to start bawling for some reason. I'm louder than Mama. The tears are streaking down, snot along with them. It takes a while for my cousins to figure out that I'm not faking.

Have you ever cried about one thing and used it as an excuse to cry even harder about another? I guess the road's served up some hard days, too, along with all the good ones. I haven't slept more than five hours straight since Cairo, and I'm worn out. If only there was a key and I could turn my mind off. I keep thinking about Maggie and Mrs. McBean and everybody else we met this summer.

"The *striving*," Mrs. McBean called it. Until now I wasn't sure what that meant, but it must be the thing that makes us wave to a stranger when we don't have to, and that gets us to clean a friend's house even though it will never be lived in again, and that keeps us looking even when we know we'll never find.

I'm also thinking about Larry and Cornell. The calls from Ball Garage have been more frequent lately, and it looks like it's time to head home. "Summers are always too short," Larry said just this morning. "How long have we been gone? Seven weeks? Eight?" He looked at the day planner on his phone and chuckled to himself. "Nine. It's been nine. Next year we should consider stretching it to twelve, but I suppose we could make it fifty-two and that still wouldn't be enough."

If I've learned one thing about my cousins, it's that Fords are just a way for them to be good to people.

"June?" Larry says now. "Why all the tears? What is wrong, son?"

I can't stop them. In fact, the more I try, the more they come down.

Cornell brakes hard, and we screech to a stop in the middle of the road. We are out in the boonies, and you can see for miles, the long ribbon of road stretching out in both directions with no cars on it. We unlatch our seat belts and pile out.

The sun burns a single white hole in the sky. The wind blows and flattens the wheatgrass in the fields. I stuff my hands in my pockets and lean my head forward, trying to keep the tears and other stuff from messing up my coveralls.

I know they wouldn't be shutting things down unless they had to. Sorry if this sounds corny, but there's a little boy who lives in me, even as I've grown up and tried to leave him behind. He's in me, making me see life the way he does even when I know I should look at it differently. He can be very immature. He can be hardheaded. He's the one who thought we could find Daddy. He's the one who wouldn't let me stop looking.

When I'm done crying, I say, "I'm sorry, but Huck needs to go. I don't like him being on the road with us." I pull myself up in the cab and grab the book. "I wouldn't want him in the library, either. I don't care if it is a bunker."

They don't answer one way or the other.

I throw the book over a fence and into a field. It sails out there, flapping around, then comes down hard. No, it doesn't go as far as Maggie threw the horse book, but who cares as long as I gave it all I had?

"Why do they even write books if they can't make them good?" I say. I climb up in the cab and straddle the shift, taking my usual position.

Larry and Cornell are still standing in the road, one looking one way, the other the other way.

"But it's supposed to be a classic," Larry says.

"Yeah, it's a classic—a classic load of crap. Let's go, cousins. Fords are waiting."

I'd figured that last part would do it. They get back in and we head out.

There's one thing about my cousins that I forgot to mention.

Whenever we're out in the sticks, they're always on the

lookout for farms selling fresh eggs. And they always seem to find them. You've seen the places I'm talking about. You're out on a little country road, kicking up a dust storm that colors the reeds in the ditches, and up ahead there's a house set back in a grove of trees. As you get closer, you see the fence that surrounds the old place, and on a post at the turn-in there's a hand-lettered sign hanging by a nail. The board isn't cut square, and time and the elements have faded the message on its face.

EGGS, it seems to say. But you could be wrong.

Larry puts his phone away and starts drawing pictures in his notebook. As usual, the view out the windshield doesn't quite match the sketch on the page. Nobody's announced it yet, but I know where we are. Even though we haven't seen many cars since we left the interstate, those we have seen have all had Wisconsin license plates.

"Hallelujah," Cornell says. He points to the lowly farmstead, and Larry does a quick sketch of eggs in a nest.

In real life the sign is hanging crooked, but in Larry's picture it hangs straight. Cornell puts on the blinker.

Something about the house is familiar. I'm not able to identify it until Larry says, "How 'bout that? Another Sears home." And I understand at last: The house is exactly like Maggie's back in Cairo. It's not like the one she shared with her grandmother, but the one where she grew up with her mom and dad.

We drive closer, and I'm glad to see there are no holes in this one, and no vines clinging to the window screens. The paint looks new: white on the board siding, green on the porch floor. The yard is clean.

Cornell stops and punches the horn, and the three of us get out. A young woman appears on the porch with a little girl hugging her leg. They stand there watching us with equal amounts of curiosity and suspicion. "We saw your sign," Cornell says. "Got any fresh brownies today?"

It's the same every time. Before she answers, I whisper, "Let me check," and then the lady repeats these same words.

She lifts the girl in her arms and follows a dirt trail along the side of the house to the backyard. I see a hay barn, a chicken coop, and an old one-car garage covered in vines and leaning badly to one side.

"You can come," the lady says, and we walk back to meet the husband.

The door to the coop stays closed as he wades in among the clucking birds and starts gathering eggs. "How many you need?" he shouts.

"How many you got?" Larry and Cornell answer. Today I make it a chorus, all three of us asking the question at the same time.

The husband is in no hurry. He loads a big rush basket, taking care to keep the shells from bumping. "Twenty-two," he shouts. "Twenty-two good?"

"Perfect," we answer.

The little girl wants to play, and her mother lets her down. The man removes the eggs from his basket and puts them on beds of straw in paper bags from a local grocery. Cornell gives him several bills folded in half. When the man reaches for his wallet to make change, Cornell holds his hand out. "No, sir. You keep that."

The girl is standing in front of me now. Like everything else about this stop, I have a feeling I've seen her before. I crouch down to put myself at her level, and she shuffles up closer. Her eyes sparkle like a river I've seen, and her smile has the future in it.

"What is your name?" she says.

"Jack," I answer. "What is yours?"

Larry and Cornell keep trying to look inside the garage. I suppose they can't see one without wondering what's in it. There are cracks in the door, but none big enough to reveal much.

"Mind if we pull the vines off and have a peek inside?" Larry says to the husband.

"Not at all," the man says. "Here, let me go get my machete from the barn. You'll never get in there just pulling."

It must take twenty minutes, the three of them chopping at the vines. Then Larry and Cornell double-team the door, pulling against it at once and groaning as they force it open. A long, golden bar of light shoots in, and there it is parked under a blanket of dirt and cobwebs, tires flat, windows busted out, waiting to be saved as all of them are.

My cousins turn back to make sure I'm seeing it.

"A Model T," they say at once, voices trembling, faces filled with awe and wonder.

TWENTY-FOUR

THIS MIGHT SURPRISE YOU, but it really hasn't been all that hard to go without technology this summer. Larry's on his phone a lot, but when he's working on a car, he often leaves it plugged into the generator. Many times I could've taken it without his knowing and watched reunion videos. I never did. Except for when I called Mama, I haven't used the phone at all.

I don't know why I'm proud of that. Maybe it's the same reason I'm proud of myself for not eating a lot of junk over the last two months. I haven't had a single chocolate-covered raisin since we left home. I'm no longer weak that way. This is something else the road has given me: power over my dinkiest self.

Looking back on it, there's one thing about those videos that always bothered me. The kid in them is played for a sucker every time, all for the moment when he spots his mom or dad and they have their reunion. He's a sucker because the mom or dad set him up, and so did everybody else. The principal and teachers at the school, the refs at the ball game, and sometimes even the spectators in the bleachers who happen to have their phones out at just the right time.

Dumb kid. He's too innocent to understand that he got played.

It's not definite yet, but I might be done with those videos.

I would say the same for cheese, but it's almost noon and we haven't had anything to eat yet.

Hey, don't do me like that!

At least cheese is real.

Our Australian navigator hasn't said a word all afternoon, but he hasn't needed to. The last road sign we drove past said SHEBOYGAN FALLS 5.

I couldn't tell you why Cornell is braking now unless one of them needs a tree to hide behind. Another long straightaway and a couple of turns and we're on Hickory Street.

"What was *that*?" Cornell says, tilting his head to hear better. The engine sputters and stops running.

They get out and start poking around under the hood, both of them stuffed in there like meat in a sandwich.

"Where . . . are . . . you?" Cornell says through gritted teeth. I'm used to this by now. He's talking to the thing that's wrong with the truck.

"Bloody bow ties," Larry says. "How much do you want to bet it was that loser again? *Lou-ee Show-zeph Shave-row-lay.* Yeah, he did it."

I slide over and sit behind the wheel. We changed the battery last week, so that can't be it. The pointer on the fuel gauge is halfway between *E* and *F*.

I can't remember the last time we filled up, but wasn't it Iowa City? If it was, there's no way we have half a tank left.

"The pointer broke," I say through the open window. "The tank's dry."

"It is not dry."

"I'm telling you it's dry. We're out of gas."

They take turns in the driver's seat booting the gauge with their fingers and trying to get the engine going. Nothing works.

"Wait till I get my hands on him," Larry says, still on Chevrolet.

"June," Cornell says, "go in back and grab a five-gallon can, will you? Cousin Larry misplaced his mind and can't seem to find it."

I do what he says, but the cans are empty, all of them. I place them side by side at the side of the road, and Larry and Cornell move from one to the next testing their weight to make sure none has any gas left.

"You didn't believe me?" I ask, pretending to be insulted.

"We believed you," Larry says.

"What we can't believe," Cornell says, "is that we got this close. Think of all the Fords we put back on the road this summer, and now on our last day, only a few miles from home, our old friend up and quits on us."

He and Larry remove three chairs from the back and

arrange them in a semicircle facing the road. If I didn't know better, I'd say they welcomed the chance to extend the journey a while longer. Next they'll be setting up the tent and the thunderbox and firing up the cookstove.

"Tell me," Cornell says, "does this prove your cousins are human, after all?"

I don't know why there's so little traffic today, but we sit for half an hour and see only a UPS van and a station wagon. The situation doesn't seem to bother Larry and Cornell, but it has me wanting to holler, and I decide to do something about it.

I grab the handle of one of the cans and start walking to town. There's a gas station not far from my house. I probably could make it there and back in an hour and a half. If I can hitch a ride, it'll be more like twenty minutes.

"Hold on there, June," Larry says. "Let me call somebody first."

He picks up the phone but doesn't make the call just yet. Instead he stands in front of me and uses his fingers to comb my hair, then he takes his thumb and wipes away a smudge on my face. He's been brushing dirt off my coveralls since Memphis, but this is taking it to a new dimension.

"You look very handsome," he says. "If you want to come with us again next summer . . ." But his voice breaks and he can't finish.

Cornell must be tired of waiting. He grabs the phone from Larry's hand and makes the call himself: "Hello, dear, it's

Cornell. Lawrence is indisposed at the moment. Listen, we've run into a problem. We ran out of gas on Ourtown Road . . . Yes, yes, we did . . . I kid you not. Better believe I am. Red as a beet . . . Hey, listen, if it's not too much trouble, do you think you could come out here with some regular unleaded? Yes, yes . . . Gas for the mower will do . . ."

When he's done the three of us go back to waiting. Cornell shakes some sunflower seeds into his mouth and manipulates them into a ball, while Larry removes a notebook from the glove box and does some drawing. Larry keeps glancing over at me, until I start to feel uncomfortable and walk over to see what he's up to. There's a kid in the picture, but I don't know him. He's taller and bonier than me. He looks like Daddy when Daddy was young. Yeah, a lot like Daddy. "It's good, but his eyes aren't quite like that," I say.

"It's you, June."

"Me?" And I move in closer.

Larry writes his initials and the date in the corner, then he hands me the notebook. I flip through it and every page has my picture, going back to our first night together. I'm sleeping with my head on Cornell's arm. I'm scraping dauber nests and raising the tent. I'm trimming a goatee and taking the carburetor apart. I'm eating and laughing and dancing.

As I turn the pages, you can see me change. I start out with a scared look on my face. By the end I have a confident one. My hair keeps getting longer. I don't have a single muscle in the beginning. I have a few in today's portrait.

"Something to remember the road by," he says. "Go on. Take it."

"Gosh, cousin, I don't know what to say."

"Then don't say anything, unless it's thank you."

"Thank you. Thank you so much."

The sun is in his face, and he squints looking up at me. "No, June, thank you."

The person with the gas finally appears off in the distance, a speck on the road getting bigger by the second. I don't figure out who it is until I recognize the pickup, and by then Larry has his phone ready. It's in video mode, and he's already begun recording.

"How could you?" I look from one cousin to the other.

The pickup stops on the other side of the road, and Daddy steps out. There's something different about him, something I've seen only in old pictures. There are no bruises from falling on his face. And Mama must've cut his hair, because it's shorter than the last time I saw him. He's how he must've looked once, back before everything that happened.

I hate to be a sucker, but in the end I'm just like all the others. He crouches and opens his arms wide, and I run to meet him.

TWENTY-FIVE

IT WAS MR. DAUTERIVE, the sheriff's deputy with the Falcon down in Louisiana, who tracked him down. They talked several times on the phone, once late at night for right at three hours, and Mr. Dauterive finally was able to convince him to go home.

Daddy had joined some other veterans from his unit on a commercial fishing boat in the Gulf of Mexico. They worked out of Bon Secour, Alabama, gill-netting mullet and Spanish mackerel, and they worked so hard day after day in the hot sun that he got sick whenever he tried to drink. After he felt better, he joined a veterans' support group, then started seeing counselors at the VA in Mobile. The first time he and Mr. Dauterive spoke, it was on a cell phone that belonged to the captain of the boat. Mr. Dauterive identified himself as a Ranger who'd met me in Pineville, Louisiana, and Daddy said, "Don't lie to me, man," and hung up.

He didn't let us know where he was because he was

ashamed. His mind had him believing we were better off without him, since he wasn't any good and wasn't worth loving. It also had him believing we didn't want him back. That might've been the craziest part, that we didn't want him back.

"Oh, he wants you back," Mr. Dauterive told him. "He's out on the road now looking for you."

OMG GUESS WHO JUST WALKED IN THE DOOR!!! Mama said in a text to Larry the same day we stopped for eggs and found the Model T.

"You were always with me," Daddy tells me at the side of the road. "I could feel you. Could you feel me, June?"

"Yes, sir."

"Sometimes I could hear your heart beating. It got louder the more I tried to tell myself it was only my heart. But it was yours, I knew it was."

"I could hear yours, too, Daddy."

Larry and Cornell let us talk for a while, then they walk over with their hands out. It's a little awkward, seeing as all they want to do is shake, but then Daddy pushes past their hands and wraps them up in his arms. He's rough about it, cupping their necks in back, pulling them close.

"Cousin Henry," they say, one after the other.

I'm just glad nobody's recording. It would be a hard thing to erase from people's minds, the three of them doing that like that out in the middle of nowhere, and all the wet sounds they make.

Not that this is big news, but we were never out of gas.

And the fuel gauge wasn't broken. Cornell did some trick to make the engine sputter, then when they got out and looked under the hood, Larry removed the ignition coil wire from the coil. That wire pops right off, and it goes back on just as easily. So I had it wrong. Look, I never once pretended to be a car genius, but at least I'm trying.

"How about pizza?" Daddy says. "Anybody hungry?"

I raise my hand and run and get in the truck—the COE truck. It's a habit, but under the circumstances it's the right thing to do. We started out together. It's only right we end together.

We go to the place next to the Déjà Do, and Mama clears her book and comes over and joins us. I sit between Larry and Cornell, and Mama and Daddy sit next to each other across from us. It's beyond strange to see them together again, the way they hold hands under the table, and how she tips her head sideways and rests it on his shoulder, smiles on their faces.

"I got after your daddy," Mama says. "You tired yet of looking like somebody in a boy band?"

I know she's talking about my hair. I could complain that I like it long, but the truth is I can't wait to feel her magic fingers again.

There's a lot of catching up to do, and it's harder than you might think, so I mostly talk about the new friends I made and the Fords they drove.

"Hold on a second there," Daddy says, making me stop in the middle of a story. "What was her name again?"

"Maggie," I answer.

"Maggie," he repeats, as if he intends to memorize it.

We order three large pizzas, all of them cheese. Before the server comes with the food, Mama says, "What about those trees with the holes in them that cars can drive through? Did you ever see any?"

"Saw a lot of trees," I say, "but not one of those."

"Those are your redwoods," Cornell says. "They're in Northern California. We didn't make it out that far west this year."

"Well, that's a shame," Mama says. "But maybe it'll turn out to be a good thing in the long run. If you see and do it all when you're only eleven, what's the point of ever being twelve?"

She says she has plans for me at the salon. She's been so busy she can't keep up. Not only could I sweep up the hair and fold the towels, but lately when the phone rings the new girl at the desk is always outside smoking, and maybe I could help schedule the appointments. Having watched Larry manage the day planner all summer, I'm confident I could do it. "You could save your money until school starts," she says. "It must be about time for a new Packers jersey. Nobody likes Aaron Rodgers anymore since he went and got all full of himself."

"I like him," I say. "Are you kidding, Mama?"

"You always did believe in second chances, didn't you, bud? Oh, by the way, you won't be able to wear those coveralls to school. That's a big zipper. You won't make it past the metal detector."

Larry and Cornell look more than just disappointed. They actually seem hurt. The trembling goatees are the giveaway.

"When you're not helping your mom, why don't you come help us at the garage?" Larry says. "Think you might like that?"

Goosebumps start popping out on my arms. I don't know why they always have to do that, unless my skin is sensitive to compliments.

"Sounds like they're both vying for your services, son," Daddy says. "Makes a father proud, I can tell you that much."

"Just do for us in the shop what you did for us on the road," Cornell says. "No digging holes for the privy, though. We got us some very nice bathrooms at Ball Garage. Nobody writes on the walls."

"Yes, sir."

"The coveralls are mandatory," Larry says, staring at Mama. "At Ball Garage? I hope you understand."

"Oh, I do," she says. "I get the coveralls, and I like how he looks in them—cute little man. I want you to know I'd be loving on you now, June, if your daddy would just let me loose for five seconds."

Later, as we're finishing up the pizza, a cricket starts chirping at our table. Daddy looks for it in the basket holding the sweeteners. He checks his pockets and Mama's purse. He even gets on the floor and pokes around under our chairs.

"Good luck with that," I tell him.

The cricket chirps again.

The server brings our check, and Daddy grabs it from the little tray before his cousins can get to it. "My turn," he tells them, even though they make a scene complaining about it.

We're in the parking lot not long after, and Daddy carries the bag with my stuff to his pickup. When all that's left is to say goodbye, you suck it up and say goodbye. "Did you have somebody water your flowers while we've been gone?" I say. I'm thinking about the petunias and begonias outside their Airstreams.

They nod. "Vinny at the shop looks after them," Larry says.

"Then they should be fine."

"Yeah," Cornell says. "Should be fine."

They get in their truck and drive off, and I'm already wishing it was next summer and we were heading out on the road again. As long as Mama and Daddy are home when I get back, I know I can go anywhere and be all right.

"It was Larry who was the cricket," I say to Daddy.

"It was? How about that? All along I thought it was Cornell."

The old truck turns at the corner, and FORD is the last thing I see.

AUTHOR'S NOTE

I'M A LOT LIKE JUNE BALL. When I was a kid, I didn't like my name. My mom and dad named me John Edmund Bradley Jr. I went by Johnny before family members started calling me John Ed. For some dumb reason John Ed stuck, even as I tried to shake it as I got older. I grew up in Louisiana, where double first names are common, but people still had trouble with mine. They called me everything from John Egg and John Head to Johnette and Jah Ned. It drove me crazy.

June and I have had similar experiences. I once ate a whole jar of mayhaw jelly in the parking lot of a grocery store. I didn't have a knife, so I used my fingers to spread the jelly on slices of bread that I'd bought in the store. Larry and Cornell weren't around to help me empty the jar and wipe out the loaf, but I didn't need them. I did it all by myself.

I'm married to a hairdresser, and I've come to admire her work even though I never gave much thought to hair until I met her. She tells me all the time that hairdressers are artists. June wants to do women's hair when he grows up, although he finds it hard to admit to Maggie and others that he has such a dream. Much like him, when I was a kid I had a secret dream, and that was to be a writer. I'm the son of a football coach who was an ex-Marine. In the world I knew back in the 1960s, something was wrong with a boy who aspired to a life in the arts. I was nineteen before I was able to confide to my mom and dad that I wanted to be a novelist. It was a painful thing to tell them, and I remember crying a little. But they were fine with it. In fact, they already knew it from how much I loved books and idolized writers. They hugged me and told me to go out and be great.

June meets Mrs. McBean when he and his cousins visit Cairo, Illinois. He learns that Mrs. McBean's husband was a newspaper reporter who died in 1969 from a gunshot wound while out doing his job. Protestors clashed with vigilantes after a young army private, Robert L. Hunt Jr., died while in police custody. This conflict really happened—it's a part of our history—but there was no Preston McBean, and no reporters died while covering the story.

The recent worldwide protests against racism and police brutality echo what happened in Cairo all those years ago. George Floyd, whose death in Minneapolis on May 25, 2020, sparked the outcry, is a modern-day Robert Hunt. I invented Mr. and Mrs. McBean to help me illustrate ideas I had about love, devotion, sacrifice, and forgiveness. Although the McBeans were not real in actual fact, they are real in spirit. There are people like them wherever you go.

In addition to writing books, I've also worked as a newspaper and magazine writer. Some of the finest people I know are journalists. They work hard to keep us informed about what's going on in the world, and sometimes they put their lives on the line. They are not the "enemy of the people," as you might've heard somebody say in recent years. Rather, they and the people are one and the same, and most of them are fair and honest.

I started my career as a reporter for the *Washington Post*, assigned to the sports department. My editors would send me out on the road to cover stories, often for weeks at a time, and wherever I went I made an effort to meet people and to make friends. This continued in the years after I left the *Post* and wrote stories for *Sports Illustrated*.

Being away from home for long periods wasn't easy, but I made it fun by connecting with strangers who were just as curious about me as I was about them. I met the kind of people June meets. I liked the stories they told, and I stored them away in my head, knowing I'd use them in my books one day. Traveling from one region to another taught me that no matter where we come from we're all basically the same and all basically good. June and I discovered America the same way, by going out on the road and throwing our arms around it.

I hope you have the chance to experience the country the way he and I did. Sure, you might have a flat tire or two along the way, but you'll learn how lucky you are to be an American.

ACKNOWLEDGMENTS

ONE DAY SEVERAL YEARS AGO I told my friend Del Segura about a dream I'd had. A big tree was growing in the bed of an old pickup truck. The truck had been abandoned and left to rot in a field, and the tree had taken root in some dirt in back and grown to full size.

Del is a race car driver who also happens to have a PhD in mechanical engineering.

The pickup in my dream was a Ford, and when I told Del this he said there were people out in the country who knew everything about old Fords and were always searching for rare models. Del called these people "Ford men." He took his phone out of his pocket and said he would make a call if I was interested in talking to one.

"Ford men?" I said.

"Yeah. If the car's rare enough they'll travel to you for a look at it. They'll also repair it for you. These guys are obsessed."

He told me there were others whose passion began and ended with Chevrolet. "Chevy men," Del called them.

The Ford men and the Chevy men were friendly rivals.

This is how a book begins—with a dream, an image, a notion. I left Del and went home and started writing.

I've already thanked Del a thousand times for introducing me to the world of Ford men, but it's still not enough. I'm equally indebted to my agent, Esther Newberg. I showed her some early pages featuring Larry and Cornell Ball and she in turn showed them to Wesley Adams at Farrar Straus Giroux. It was Wes who originated the idea of a boy traveling the roads one summer with the eccentric Ball cousins. Until Wes suggested making the book a coming-of-age story, June Ball did not exist.

So thanks to Del, Esther, and Wes. Without them this book would not have been written.